Message From the Author

Hi there! Thank you for taking the time to read <u>Moon Thief.</u> I would like to share more good deals, free books, and stories with you. Currently, I'm sending fans a free author video reading of another of my books. Just sign up at www.pgshriver.com to receive your free video. Better be quick though. I hear there are only so many free downloads available!

Have an enlightened day!

Hardcover Edition
ISBN: 978-1-952726-24-8

Address comments and inquiries to:

Gean Penny Books
Axtell, TX 76624

info@geanpenny.com
author@pgshriver.com

Internet URL: http://www.pgshriver.com

Acknowledgements

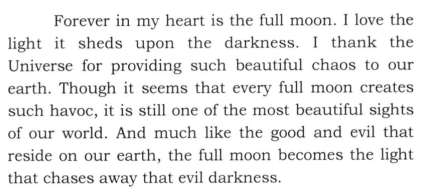

Forever in my heart is the full moon. I love the light it sheds upon the darkness. I thank the Universe for providing such beautiful chaos to our earth. Though it seems that every full moon creates such havoc, it is still one of the most beautiful sights of our world. And much like the good and evil that reside on our earth, the full moon becomes the light that chases away that evil darkness.

I acknowledge the Greater Power beyond for sharing such beauty with me that I felt compelled to write this book about it.

This book is dedicated to the three

dearest M's in my life

Mikayla

Miranda

Mom

A Letter From Moon Child

Before you read my story, I want you to know that I'm okay.

I was not overtaken by greed— or chocolate chip cookies. I have problems, like you, and one of them is Mean Child. He earned that name because he's a bully. He has always been one. He had that name before we became brothers.

My life is surrounded by love and purpose. I am different, yes. Different from you, or your best friend, or even your worst enemy. I am different, and I accept that I am different, because through those differences, I've found my purpose in this world, and my purpose makes me happy. I am comfortable being me, even though I can never see the sun, or have friends.

I could change my world, but I choose not to because I enjoy my simple life, my life of moon power, my life of friendships as different as I. I have the power to change the world, but I don't.

You also have the power to change the world, but should you? Are the changes you seek to make in your world good or bad for those around you? Will the changes you make produce good feelings in your community, in your world? Or will people in your community dislike those changes?

Before you use your powers to change your world, ask yourself, is that change necessary? Will it make you happier in the long run? Will it make other people happy? Before you make that change, read my story.

In my community, people are happy with their lives, their jobs, their families. They don't desire change, or technology, or chocolate chip cookies, no matter what someone else might think.

You might think our world would be better if we had what you have, but I tell you now that we did have what you had and this new world is what came from the destruction of yours.

Before you read my story, I want you to know that I am living in your future, one that was born of the world you now live in, one that I choose to keep as it is— forever.

Moon Child

Run! Run, Moon Child, run! The coyotes are right behind you! Hurry, you must get away! They will kill you, too! Run!

I ran, fast as the wind in a storm I ran. I could not let Coyote catch me. Why would one who had for so long been my friend hunt me?

Wait. Who called me? Who told me to run? Nobody cared but Mother, and that is not Mother's voice. I stopped. I turned warily. Another like me stared into my face. The Moon glow of the forested background in which he stood changed to black.

Through the darkness, up from the ground below me, tall shining structures formed around him where monstrous trees once stood. Huge structures where the sun shone from each window in spite of the darkness.

"Who are you? Why do you have me run from my friend?"

Other me stared back, silent as a reflection in a pool of water, calm, smooth, no rippling. Fear overtook me again, for I did not understand, nor did I know where I was, what ground I stood upon.

The forest disappeared in the midst of this huge glimmering village, one larger, grander than any I had ever seen. People rushed everywhere about this boy look-a-like and me. Some people waved at him from inside moving domes, some as long as ten of our domes put together, but flat on top, with many, many people inside. The large domes rolled past, gliding upon a hard surfaced path wide enough for thirty villagers to walk upon, hands joined, arms outstretched.

They all smiled at me. Me, who had not one single human friend in the village; they did not point and laugh, nor did they call me names, yet I was afraid of this place, this magic.

I was not allowed to go out and play, not like the other children in our village. I could not shine as they did, in games like Sneak Away, Top of the Hill, and Rock Brigade. I could hear them out in the village, after chores, their joy, their terror, their fun filling the warm morning. At some mystical point before I would arise, one of them would wake me, crying over a misplaced rock, an accidental shove, an early catching.

I always imagined that, if I were allowed to go outside with them and shine, that crying child would be me. Then I would get all of the attention of the working mothers who looked on as the children of the village played and learned skills for their future jobs and responsibilities in the village.

In the village, crying was not a sign of weakness, but strength, unless the people could not see you cry, like me, during the day when all the other children shone their skills to everyone, and I, stuck inside, lay in my bedroll trying to sleep, tears wetting my folded arms beneath my head.

It was not because my mother had no husband, and would not take a new one after my father's death. Although a single woman in the village was not considered a good omen for the village. A woman was expected to choose a new husband within six months after the loss of one husband. Someone had to take care of her and her children, which in our case was only me.

It has been almost twelve moons since my father died. In just twelve days, it will be twelve moons. I remember, because he disappeared on the day which celebrates my birth, and I will have seen twelve Moons, twelve times on that day.

Father had left the village early that morning, in search of a special gift for me, which I never received. He and mother had argued late the previous night over the gift. They did not think I heard because I had already left the dome to play. I remember the pat on the head, his rough hand on my cheek as he left the village.

It has been very difficult for my mother to choose a new husband because she loved my father so much. She will never find another like him, she says. I miss my father. But that is not why I cannot join the others in their games of skill.

My father used to tell me how special I was, how someday I would be amazing and the people of all the villages would see me shine. I was chosen for this suffering because I was to be great one day. I would do something so amazing that the entire world would remember my name, Moon Child.

Mother would nod, her arm locked in father's as she wiped away my tears with her free hand, all the children laughing and squealing outside, soaking up the morning sunshine, just beyond the row of rough earth domes where our people spent their nights, all the people except for me. My nights were my days.

I remained in our earthen dome all during the day, trying to sleep with all the happy child voices just beyond my reach.

Happy dreams planted inside my head of days spent outside, shining like the other children, hiding behind domes and bushes, playing village games.

I would wake up at first dark, my bedroll wet with tears where my head lay in the day, the enormous, round, silver Moon shining down upon me through the small window of my space, making my skin glow, comforting my melancholy. It was the only time I ever shined, every Moon night at this time, the Moon smiling down upon me, but no one ever saw me shine. No one.

I shone like the Moon itself, more than any other child did in any village anywhere, and no one saw me. No longer was my skin pale, nearly translucent, but it was thick and bright and beautiful and strong. I didn't know what I would do if the Moon was not there at all to see me shine, to make me shine. All my life, the Moon has been there, peeking through the tiny window, waking me, calling me, asking me to come out and shine. And I do. Every Moon night, while the villagers sleep, I do.

Mother awoke the first time I was old enough to leave; she smiled, waved and then returned to sleep. My parents always slept at night; they had day chores, like normal villagers.

Of course, no children sang songs or played games or climbed rock solid trees outside the village when I left my dome. But I did have some friends— not human— but friends. Other Moonchildren like me, who mostly roamed at night, when the Moon was full and high in the near black sky. Coyotes, raccoons, owls, bats all came out to greet me and watch me shine. They knew my strength. They played with me and spoke to me, though not human games or words. We communicated with our eyes, our actions and our hearts. We were of the night, and the Moon contributed her bright light so that we could play. She smiled at our antics, our games of tag, our discoveries of her hidden secrets, like the Moonflower.

Every Moon Night, I watched the Moonflower open, its soft white petals glowing, so delicate, like me. I would hold my slender finger close to its petals, comparing my skin to the tiny surface. Then, gently, I would stroke the soft petal, its layers so smooth, and it would quiver beneath my touch, as though delighted to have a friend who cared so much about it. Someone who would not trample it under foot. Someone who understood its near magical essence. It made me happy, yet lonely for others like myself. I wished that I had magical powers, too.

So I guarded the delicate flower, as my parents guarded me. Never once did I consider plucking the tiny flower from its home. I understood that it would die if I did. It would no longer be there for me.

Only one of these tiny flowers existed beyond our village. I wondered about its lonely life, why others did not grow around it. We had so much in common, the Moonflower and I, especially our lonesomeness. Every Moon Night, I lay next to it, telling it of my troubles, my pain, my grief.

Like the night my father died. All that night, while the Moon filled the sky with light, the Moonflower listened while I cried, watering its gentle surface with my own salty tears.

Mother had come out that night, because she could not sleep. She worried she would lose me, too. She stood in awe of the Moonflower, of its stunning beauty, not understanding that her own beauty equaled that of the flower, only opposite. Her dark hair glimmered in the bright light sifting through the trees and her deep, blue eyes, so unlike my own pale ones, danced with the Moon. We made a pact that night that I would not go beyond the Moonflower, just outside the village, so she could hear me, and wake in the night to save me, should something happen.

But one night, while silver Moon beams rippled through the gently blowing trees, tiny lights dancing as though playing with my friends and I, I did not keep that pact.

2

On that evening, I lay beside my Moon friend, on my back, my arms bent, pillowing my head, and stared up at the flickering lights that danced as tiny leaves on slender arms swayed in the breeze, our own light show, music in the wind and night sounds. From the corner of my eye, I watched a beam cast down upon my friend, and though other lights danced around from rock to grass to clover, this light remained, brighter, thicker and stronger than the rest, a lifeline to the tender flower, feeding its beauty.

I sat up and watched the flower, and it was at peace, as if smiling. My gaze followed the beam upward to the Moon, searching the source, and spotted another such beam, much wider, shooting out from the Moon, touching down softly somewhere beyond the tall forest. *More Moonflowers*, I thought excitedly, and jumped from my seat on the soft brown earth to follow the large beam.

My friend is not alone! I hesitated at the remembrance of the pact, but curiosity and excitement led my heart and urged me onward.

It's not that far, I told myself, justifying my reasons for breaking the pact.

Tomorrow I will ask Mother if I can further my boundaries and go beyond the flower. After all, I am almost twelve.

I ran, swift as Coyote through the darkly lit forest, hoping the beam would remain as a guide. In each clearing, I stopped; I followed with my eyes the destination of the beam, and its closeness to my new position, but it seemed to grow further away each time. like the ends of the brightly colored arcs in the sky I've heard other children search for after a rain.

Further I ran, swiftly jumping fallen trees, skirting thorny bushes, and stepping soundless, as taught.

A motion drew my eyes away from the invisible path I ran, a motion to my left, four legs, high bushy tail, long snout. My friend, the Coyote, smiled as he ran with me, tongue lolling.

Knowing my destination, he led the way, several lengths ahead. He guided me toward the light, pushing me on, increasing my speed, keeping me from harm. I felt free, free of my constraints of the day, free of the pain of the anniversary of my father's death, free of the difference that was me.

I worried not about the end of the path, for I knew it must be Moonflowers, hundreds of thousands of Moonflowers!

It gave me hope. For if there were more Moonflowers, then certainly there were more like me, Moonchildren, playing games in the night.

Perhaps a village lay at the end of my flight, an entire village of Moon people, and mother and I could move to that village, where I could be happy and never again lonely. She would be happy, too, because she was not bound by the day. She could survive in the night or the day, unlike her son. She would be happy, because I would be happy.

My heart soared as my leather tough feet bounded through the hopes and dreams I created around the huge beam of light and the village that must lie at its end, but my breath came quicker now, and the light seemed just as far away.

Coyote stopped before me at a stream, understanding I needed to catch my breath. I had run far on my dreams, and my heart was anxious to continue, but my body was tired, so I rested, I drank, I slowed my breathing, and then Coyote ran again, and I followed.

I watched the Moon as it sank a little lower in the western half of the black sky, fearing I would not make it home before dawn, before the burning sun would fill the earth and scorch me raw.

Perhaps I should turn around, I doubted. *I will never reach the moonlighted village I have dreamed of, for I am too slow,* I scolded.

But then, Coyote yipped, high and loud over his shoulder, to draw my attention from my concerns to the recipients of the Moon beam. I slowed before the edge of the forest, unable to believe the sight before my eyes. My heart sank as my fantasy crumbled before me, yet something amazing happened, and I an only witness, except Coyote, who lay before me smiling, the rhythm of his pant matching that of my own.

One lone shelter, a white glimmering dome as white as Moon itself, stood before my eyes, but surrounding it were millions of tiny white, beautiful Moonflowers, and at their center, just beyond the entrance to the dome, stood a woman, a woman like me, a Woman of the Moon.

Her arms rose and fell, from Moon to the ground below, as a frail bird, and from her fingertips, soft rays of moonlight guided the two beams I had seen to their destination. I remained quiet, invisible to the woman in trance like concentration, arms flowing up and down, the wings of her white gown rising and falling with the motion, as Owl's wings in flight.

Momentarily, she paused, as if sensing my presence, then she continued, a soft chant emitting from her thin, aging lips. I wanted to move forward, to hear the words erupting softly from her throat, as though I should know them, but I feared trampling the Moonflowers she danced so lightly through. The tiny flowers seemed to cover the earth from her dome to the forest wall, all the way around. So as not to disturb the spell she cast, I began the trek around her dome, at the edge of the Moonflowers, my amazement growing with each step, each vision of the fluorescent field, and each enchanting word that fell on the night.

Seemingly, I walked an eternity at the edge of the beam shining down upon the Moonflowers, around the tiny dome, in the darkness. When first I reached my starting point, her song stopped and she whispered harshly, demanding, "Come closer, Moon Child! Quickly!" then, sensing my fear of trampling the beauty surrounding her, she added, "You, and only you beside myself, cannot harm the Moonflowers in any way; now come!" she ordered, motioning with her delicate, wrinkled, shining hand, directing a tiny beam down upon me.

My first step into the circular field of light was gentle. The delicate flowers beckoned my caution in walking; they were so beautiful and small. I found, however, that the lady did not lie. I could not harm the tiny flowers. As I tried to separate them, my foot seeking the earth beneath, I found I could not penetrate the area below or between them. Closing my eyes, I lifted my foot. "Stop stalling, and come now!" she urged.

Sensing the importance of my speed, I quickly released my foot to the gravity below and took another step. Below me, the Moonflowers stood tall, untouched, not felt by my bare feet. I did not walk on the Moonflowers, nor between them, but above them. I ran in happiness to the strange woman, the woman like me, noticing that she too, fairly floated above the flowers while she danced and swayed.

I looked up into her face, tiny shadowy cracks filling the brightness. "You know my name?"

She laughed softly, then stroked my pale hair with one slender hand and lifted my white chin to hold my pale eyes with her *own*. She was very old.

"Of course, silly child. How do you think you got your name?"

My eyes widened at her words. In my village, the custom for Naming has always remained the same, for thousands, upon thousands of Moons.

Only a true living great relative could name the new children, and only after a full Moon, so as to learn the destiny of the baby through meditation.

This meant, of course, that this woman before me, this woman like me, this aging woman, was my true relative, my Namer. Mother had told me of her many times, how she had disappeared from the village shortly after my birth, and nobody could find her. Often times, elderly members of the village, ailing from age, would wander away to die, feeding the cycle of life beyond the village. Only those who died in tragedy and heroics earned the honor to burial burning, for their own flesh became too sacred for feeding the cycle.

This shining woman before me I had believed dead all these years; yet here she stood, holding my chin, smiling into my gaze, glowing like the Moonflowers around her. Her warm, brilliant touch filled my skin with the light that she herself drew from the shimmering Moon, my own being becoming a part of the beam, which had led me here.

"You are my great grandson. I am your father's grandmother, Keeper of the Moonflowers, Feeder of Night Light. You are the same. Thank you, my friend, Coyote, for leading him safely to me," she called toward the lone scavenger, who whimpered impatiently. In response, she flung an outstretched arm toward the waiting beast, a single Moonbeam flowed from her fingers, floating to him a shimmering treat which seemed to defy gravity; he caught it and off he ran, yipping his joy.

"Come. We haven't much time; half the night is past. You, nor I, neither one will enjoy what happens at dawn. Follow me," she turned away and rounded the hut in the opposite direction from which I had come. I obediently followed.

3

And the pact followed me, in my thoughts and heart, yet I knew Mother would be just as excited as I when I revealed to her the secret of the Moon Lady, for she was our only living relative, my Namer, and we had presumed her dead. I couldn't wait to tell Mother of my discovery!

But soon, cursed as I had been to live my life alone as in secret, I found that this too must remain undisclosed.

"Now, before I share with you the truths of our

existence, we must perform the Secrecy Ceremony, for you mustn't tell anyone of the Moonflowers or the Moon beams or me, as this would create grave danger for all we know."

She led me to a large stone with many pictures, many messages, guides for what was to come. Disappointment darkened my face. For Mother, who had taught me how to read many of these signs in the earthen floor of our dome, would have been so happy to share this with me.

Soon Moon Lady looked upon me, a wispy, saddened smile of recognition dawning her face and, as if reading my thoughts, she encouraged, "It is difficult for one so young to live such a lonely life as the one planned out for you, but it is a great life of fulfillment, one that gives more joy than sharing the secret can bring to you or I. We do have each other, however, to share with. No one, aside from we two, may know of these miracles that you are about to learn. No one but you may know of the lessons you will be given by me over the next twelve nights up to your twelfth birthday. Hold out your hands to me, palms up."

I did as she instructed, standing by the upright large, flat, gray stone with the many instructions, most in a language I did not know, and which appeared fixed upon another flat stone at its base, the one my bare feet touched now, cool and warm at the same time beneath my feet.

She pulled a reed of thick grass from several others stuck in a hole born into the rock from thousands of years of rainwater dripping, drilling, and digging into its surface. The thick reed held out before her, one end in each hand, she smiled down at me, a smile of pride so unfamiliar to me that my eyes watered with joy. "Repeat after me the sacred words I give you now so the Secrecy Ceremony may be complete and we may begin your lessons."

We began, my voice following hers, my puzzlement increasing with each phrase, "Through these teachings, I will learn of my destiny, why I was chosen for this, the keeping of the Moon Secrets, Keeper of the Night, and Protector of the Sacred Moonflowers. Although the numbers of the Moon People are few and scattered..." at this my voice stopped, for until now, I had thought we were the only two in the world, but there were others, others like me, in far off villages performing the same tasks, the same work that was one day to be mine, that was now hers. Moon Lady waited while I took in this news, and then caught my eyes with hers, her look telling me of my misunderstanding, yet urging me on, "...throughout the years, I realize the danger of sharing these teachings with any other than the next Moon Person to follow me. Grave and tragic events will arise at my deception should I decide to share the Secrets of the Moon. A great changing will occur, for the Moon Thief will come and the Moon will be no more if he discovers these secrets."

Even as I repeated these words, belief was difficult, for I looked up at the huge, shimmering orb in the sky, my friend and companion all these many lonely nights, and could not even fathom somebody able to steal it away. How could that be? Even so, I would do what I had to do to keep my friend from being stolen from the sky, even keeping secrets from my mother, even breaking our pact.

Once again linked to my mind currents, the Moon Lady responded, "All things are possible, especially the impossible. Now, do you understand this oath that you have taken, the dangers that lurk beyond if the truths happen into the wrong hands?"

"Yes, I think so," I replied uncertainly.

With my confirmation, she took the thick reed she had been holding over my upturned palms, and with a swift movement, sliced both of my palms open as she ran it across the tender white flesh. I cried out in horror at my own blood, dripping, splashing, and staining the rock I stood upon. My own, purplish, black blood, that which I had never seen before, that flowed from my palms freely as I watched in shock.

"Quickly now!" Moon Lady grabbed my wrists and swung them out over the Moonflowers, "Turn your palms down," she instructed.

I stood dumbfounded, anticipating stains that

would forever ruin the beauty of the Moonflowers below my hands, but I was surprised to see tiny beams of light shooting up from the minute pedals into the palms of my hands. Before even one drop could fall from my hands, the beams whisked closed the wounds in my palms, turning the slices into tiny five point flowered scars that I now stared at in amazement. Surely, I must have fallen asleep next to the Moonflower beyond my village and was now dreaming.

"Though you have suffered much pain and loneliness, your heart has remained true. Only the true of heart, heart of the Moon People, can earn the mark of the precious Moonflower. You are now truly a child of the Moon, chosen to succeed me at my time of never more."

She took both of my palms, facing up now, and kissed each one gently, as if in worship, and then she turned both of her palms up to me and nodded.

I looked at the tiny Moonflower scars on her palms, identical to mine, and back into her face, a smile beaming from my confusion, and then I kissed each of her scars in return. I was no longer alone in my night. I need not fear not playing, not learning for a new job with the other village children, for I had a job. I had a destiny. But more than that, I had someone else like me.

"Come, sit with me, Grandson, and have your first lesson," I looked up at sinking Moon, worried about getting back to my village, to my home, before the dawn. "There's still time. Come," she glided over the Moonflowers to a spot behind her dome and sat amongst them, brilliant white upon white, beauty upon beauty, peacefulness aglow and surrounding us. I sat opposite her.

"I know you have many questions, as did I at

your age when I began to learn the Secrets of the Moon, but you must be patient. You will learn one lesson each night until your twelfth birthday, and this is your first. Be mindful of the Moonflower and its powers, as you have seen. Conceal its truth from all mankind; for greed of their doing can undo and bring the wrath of the Moon Thief should anyone else know of this truth."

I thought of the Moonflower outside my village then, my mother, who knew of its existence. Afraid, I squeaked out, "But my mother..."

"Your mother has forgotten the night she saw the Moonflower. As all mothers, she believes that you, having the nature of a child, picked that too beautiful Moonflower and brought its full fragrance to your nose as any other child would do when a flower comes into sight.

"Besides, your mother suffers not from the greed of mankind, or she would have married the wealthiest man in the village long ago when he chose her," she nodded, closing her eyes. "But you must remember, not all people have good hearts, good intentions, as your mother does. In fact, many hide the evil side of their hearts quite easily. But you cannot be fooled. Protection of the Moonflowers is the most important lesson you can learn, and that is your first. Do not show anyone its beauty or its power."

"But the Moonflower outside the village?" I looked around at those surrounding us.

"I gave it to you, for your comfort while you endured the lonely life you've lived, to give you another to connect with, to bring you to me at the right time. Sadly, no others can grow there, for they can only be grown for purpose, and one was enough for this purpose. It will suffer loneliness, as you do," she smiled again. "You must protect that treasure from other people. Moonflowers must not be picked and are vital to the life of Moon and the people it chose to save. It is your charge, now. That is your job in the village, a job that will prepare you, one that you must never tell anyone about, for nobody has ever known of the Moon People and their jobs, their importance to the world as it is. No one must ever know."

She looked sternly into my eyes, eyes that were at that moment assuring her that I would never tell anyone of our existence. Having such an important task after feeling for so many years that I would not have one at all increased my resolve to keep this powerful secret.

"Good. Now, a small bite to eat, and you should be on your way," she flicked open her hand, and there appeared the most magnificent white apple I had ever seen. In fact, it was the only white apple I had seen and the sweetest I had ever tasted.

"Food of the Moon," she grinned at my pleasurable moans.

Once finished, I wiped its sweet juice from my lips, wishing for another, but somehow understanding that one was enough to relish its sweetness and greed for another would make its taste bitter.

"Hurry now, and be home before dawn. Coyote will take you back. Do not stop along the way, or get side tracked or playful with any creatures;

there isn't time."

Jumping up from my soft place in the Moonflowers, I thanked my great grandmother. I promised to return the next night for the next of my lessons, and ran like the wind with a much lighter step than I carried on my trip out to the field. I followed Coyote without rest or want, until I reached the outskirts of my village, only one hour before dawn.

5

I stopped by the Moonflower, the beam now gone from its tiny surface, in a dream like state, and as if all had not been real, yet to prove it was, I tried to step on the Moonflower, and found I stepped above it, as before. I stuck my hands out beneath the light of Moon, and surely, brandished into my palms were the tiny scars, the Moonflower scars, glowing back into the light. As the first smoke of the village circled up from the holes in the tops of the earthen domes, I walked into my home, and for the first time in my life, did not cry while I listened to the children of the village playing outside. I had purpose.

"You made it just in time to help with breakfast. My goodness, have you been running? You're all winded! Sit down, now! Tell me, what excitement has caused this?" My mother motioned to the hard packed dirt floor across from her, where my blanket was folded and waiting. I sat upon it, stalling, not knowing what to tell her, not wanting to lie to her, but I could not tell her the truth.

"I had a game of tag with Coyote, Mother. He's becoming very friendly with me, like a village dog."

"Well, I have told you to be very careful with Coyote, for he can become angry and hurt you. What do you think happened to all of the village dogs here? Coyote and his pack. Tag or not, and I do know you long for someone to play with at night, you must be cautious with him."

"Yes, Mother."

I bit into one of the soft, sweet flat cakes she

prepared and sipped the strong herbal tea that the Herb Grower in the village told my mother to give me to make my skin strong. Its bitterness contradicted the sweetness of the cake, but it was soothing. The steam floated up through my nose, veiling the details of the night before and relaxing my already tired muscles.

Mother turned away, her back facing me as she looked out the window at the falling Moon. I sensed she had something to tell me, something important, and the sensation paused my chewing, the flat morsel lying on my tongue, awaiting its own demise.

"I have something to tell you, Moon Child. It may or may not be good, to you. The One Without has chosen me," her eyes found her feet.

"The One Without? You mean...?" I chewed. I knew him through the morning talk of the children outside my dome window. His name had changed, as did mother's, when his wife had died. He had a son. His son was very cruel to the other children, but through his cruelty, he had not realized that he made them shine more, and he less. He had become frowned upon by the villagers as one without purpose, as his father was one without mate.

"Yes," she turned toward me. "I must accept. No others have offered since the last I turned away. The Wise One will not wait longer," morosely she gazed upon me. "The match is good, they tell me, as we both have one without purpose."

Her eyes gleamed with tears, tears of fear, tears of longing for my father, tears of having to follow village orders.

I almost cried out in my anger and told her that her son had purpose, and then I remembered Moon Lady's instructions and bit down hard on my lower lip, nearly drawing blood. I felt drained, a terrible pain filling my heart at the words, which stung so harshly, the thoughts of the villagers voiced through my own mother. I turned away from my half-eaten breakfast and looked toward my bed. "When?" I whispered.

She hesitated in answer. "Before the twelfth celebration of your coming. Before the twelfth

Moon of your father's death. Before I disappear into Nothingness. Too soon," my mother's sad whisper echoed through the early dawn.

She gulped her sorrow.

All of the Ones Without in the village eventually disappeared into Nothingness, as did the old, if they did not take a mate.

The Moon Lady had disappeared into Nothingness, as I would at some later point in my life. I had a different understanding of Nothingness now, but I could not share it because I could not tell Mother about Moon Lady.

I turned back to her solemn form, placed my hands upon her shoulders, and lightly kissed both her cheeks, as was the custom of the blessing. She smiled weakly down into my face, then in a desperate attempt to hold on to our lives, almost a begging of forgiveness, she fiercely wrapped me in a hug and lightly kissed my fair forehead.

6

It was with heaviness of heart that I went to the Moon Lady the next night. It was then she taught me of the healing properties of the Moonflower, some of which I had experienced through the healing of my palms.

You must at all times keep the powers of the flower to yourself. No one shall know of the flower's true properties. Above all, you must not use any of its powers out of greed. The healing power is one of the strongest, and you must be wary of this one. As you have seen in your own palms, it heals quickly, but performed incorrectly, there could be repercussions, too.

These words repeated through my mind on my journey home. I memorized all the Moon Lady taught me on my journey with Coyote. I memorized all the secrets, but did not take them to heart, as I should. I protected the Moonflower. Nobody knew of its existence, but when my test of this lesson came, I made my decision without a second thought. I could not let the Knowing go through with the plans it seemed to be making.

Mother became very ill several nights before the Joining. The One Without came to see her, coaxing her wellness. The Herb Lady came every night, the aroma of fresh herbs preceding her entry, the scents of the teas she brewed filling the small dome. I looked around the tiny room from Mother's bedside, while Herb Lady steeped and brewed one after another of her healing concoctions, Mother lying beneath several blankets of hide and woven vines meant to stop the tremors that shook her body.

The dome seemed to have shrunk a great deal in my growth. I wondered how four people would fit in here for meals, sleeping and learning. It was the custom of our village for the male Joiner to move into the home of the female Joiner. All of the women in our village were builders. Mother had not had time to expand our dome, and I had never been taught how, being a boy.

I sat staring, and in my mind's eye I filled my tiny dome with the bodies of two others, placing them in their rightful forms of the tiny room, when Herb Lady brought more tea.

"I hope this works, for your sake," she peered knowingly at me, her blue eyes dull and saddened. "Certainly your mother has told you what happens when a member of the village dies with such illness?" she questioned.

"My mother is dying?"

"Well, only the Knowing really knows, but if she does, do you know what will happen?"

"No, I guess we never got around to that lesson, her being so young and well," I was afraid to ask the question seeing the concern in those oceanic eyes.

"If I cannot heal her, if she dies from this sickness, the village won't take any chances with it spreading. Your dome will be burned, with her inside of it, and all your belongings. And you, you will be inside of it, too. You will go to the Burning and be no more."

"But, Burning is an honor reserved for the brave?" I brightened somewhat, although what I knew of Nothingness was extremely better than Burning.

Herb Lady shook her head, "Not when the burning is of an entire family."

"And I could not choose Nothingness instead?"

For it had crossed my mind that I might be better off living with Moon Lady, anyway, instead of the One Without and his son without purpose. I would much rather disappear into Nothingness than be burned without honor, too. If I were burned, who would keep the Secrets of Moon? Who would protect the Moonflowers? My head bowed with the burden of this knowledge, Mother's hand hot and dry in mine.

At dark, after Herb Lady had once again brought Mother's fever low, I sneaked out of the dome. Low snores and dream moans filled the night air, drifting from the dome windows of the village. I crept as a thief in the darkness, heart heavy, as one who was leaving an entire village empty of souls. No eyes followed me.

The Moonflower glowed in recognition, and I smiled, though not inside. I was sure it was wrong, what I did. It went against what I had learned from Moon Lady. I stroked the tiny petals of the white flower, and then I stood, as a warrior brave and true, holding my hands directly above the flower, scarred palms downward, fingers tight and cupped for gathering.

I was not sure that I could succeed in my plan.

I had never drawn from the power of the flower; I had only watched as Moon Lady did. While I spoke from the center of my soul the words I needed to say, eyes closed and heart saddened, I felt a prickle of heat warming my palms. I opened my eyes to see tiny rays from the flower dancing and twirling around the star patterns. I cupped my hands again, as if holding the Moon between them, and light gathered between my fingers, my palms, a bright ball of cool brilliance filling my hands.

I moved my hands closer and the ball became smaller. I moved them away from each other, and the ball of light became larger. Within this ball of light was the essence needed to heal my mother and keep me from my Burning, but my heart became heavy with grief as I struggled for reasoning in my decision to directly disobey Moon Lady's teachings. Was this a time to use the healing powers of the Moonflower, or did I use it out of greed? I did not know. The answer would not come as I played with the ball of light, expanding it and shrinking it. How much light did I need? How much would it take to heal her?

I took the long way around the village with the light so as not to draw attention from those who might have the night wanders. The Moon darkened with clouds, and the risk was high of the unexpected light awakening villagers, so I shielded the ball with my body as often as I could. Creeping into the dome, the shining ball before me, I knelt before my mother's weak body. I knew not what to do, holding the ball above my mother, to use it for healing. I just knelt there, the ball of light suspended from my fingertips above her, waiting for my intuition to guide me. The light from the ball filled the tiny dome and I worried that rays shot from the small windows, too, awakening the village with wonder.

Suddenly, the ball left my fingers, floated gently down to my mother's forehead, and broke apart, flowing like tiny rivers dazzling, sparkling brightest smoke into every crevice of my mother's head, her nostrils, her mouth, and her ears, taking a miniscule lifetime to dissipate and leave us once again in the dark.

No longer did I hold the ball of light between my palms and a flash of guilt flooded my heart. I had not even the time to make the decision to heal her, as the light made it for me. I brought it here, to my dome, to my sick mother's side, and it decided to heal her.

I did not let go; it fairly floated to her head and dispersed. I knelt in saddened shock at my selfish actions while my mother peacefully rested, a glimmer of a smile on her face, tiny beads of sweat pricking her brow and her heart aglow with health.

The urge to seek out the Moonflower overcame me, to lie next to it on the cool earth and gaze at its beauty, to stroke its bright petals lightly, to smell its delicate fragrance, but I had taken its power for myself without even knowing how. I was certain now that my choice to use its power was the wrong one. An image from the sky, the Moonflower wilting away, dying alone in the forest because its power of light had been stolen so greedily, pushed me out the door and into the night once again, but this time without regard for open eyes or nosey ears, for tears of death clouded my sight and clogged my hearing.

I reached the edge of the forest, but did not immediately find the Moonflower in its home on the surface. Stumbling about, crying desperately into the cool night air, I grabbed my head and began to chant while I moved through the shrubbery about the edge of the forest. Tears traveled in tiny rivers on my cheeks, small rafts in white water. I could not find it. It was gone! I had killed my first and only friend with my greed.

In my confused and self-tormented state, I hadn't realized that I had entered at the wrong opening to the forest, for as I clumsily moved about in my grief, there, thirty feet away, my friend stood proud and bright, begging my attention, tiny rays of light coaxing praise for a service well fulfilled from the one who had taken from it so readily.

I fell at the side of the Moonflower, begging forgiveness, and there I watered its delicate stem from my own hot tears until a hand touched my shoulder, startling me to my feet. I had been followed! How could I be so stupid? I would never fulfill my purpose, now! I turned toward the hand; head lowered with shame, excuses and lies filling my thoughts.

7

"Moon Child, what is it? Why do you cry so?" a familiar voice found its way through the thickness of sorrow. My eyes snapped up with relief.

"Moon Lady!" I cried, wrapping my arms about her waist, burying my damp face into the folds of her flowing white robe, atoning for my wrong doings.

She patted my back gently with one withering hand, while stroking my pale hair with the other.

"What is it, Grandson? What troubles you? I knew you suffered last night when you came for your lesson, and tonight when you did not return, I came to you. What is it, Moon Child?"

"I have done a terrible thing," I choked, my harsh words muffled by her softness.

"How so?" I could feel her smile through the gentle question, so I withdrew, raising my weeping eyes to her smiling ones.

"I have stolen from the flower," the image of our feet, toe to toe, filled my vision. "Mother was ill, very ill... the Burning was upon us... I did not know what to... I could not let her die... failed," broken explanations between sobs surrounded us.

"Oh, Moon Child," Moon Lady lifted my eyes to hers again, her soft, wrinkled hands cupping my tear stained face on either side, her thumbs wiping my dampened cheeks, compassion in her heart. "You have not failed. You did what your heart begged you do. I told you, you are of pure heart, and when you follow your heart, you cannot wrong Moon. The healing powers of the

Light are to be used exactly in that way, silly boy!"

Her warm smile calmed my heart; her words soothed my guilt away. "You truly are a child of the Moon. You have drawn the power of the flower from its core with no practice and little guidance. Only the truest and most powerful Moon Children can do so. Be proud, child! Be proud of your quick thinking and strong heart! Your mother will live on and you shall fulfill a great purpose."

My heavy heart lifted and the clouding left my mind. I had done the right thing and Mother would live!

"Come, walk with me," she took my hand in hers and led me into the darkness of the forest. "I want to tell you a story, a story from the past, about the beginnings of the Light Ones, the Moon People. Let this be tonight's lesson, as you are such an advanced one.

"Many thousands of years ago, the people filled the earth, and many glistening structures filled the sky, the world was very different from today, and then a great war came to the world. People in every part of the world fought each other with weapons so complex, so cruel, so invasive, that most of the people died in that war, for such a terrible mist filled the air that none could hide from it.

"Structures crumbled, plants withered, and all life forms seemed lost in lingering illness and impending death.

"The mist crept into crevices and cracks so tiny that even those hiding underground were said to have perished. The Moon hid night after night from fear of being lost forever to the mist, as the mist traveled so quickly and so far.

"But, a few of the people during that Great War withstood the horrible sickness that followed the Breathing of the mist. Not of their own will, however. For next the Moon shone brightly, many, many darkened nights later, after the mist had left this world, and released Moon to the world, Moon shot its rays of light down to this devastated, dried up ball of a world. And up from a once mist filled crack shot a plant so delicate, so green in the grayness left behind, that its beauty was not lost to those last sufferers who lay dying in the dust of devastation.

"When next the Moon shone in all its fullness, a flower bloomed and drew Moon's rays unto its surrounding earth. One of the few brave and dying crawled toward the beauty and brightness of the tiny flower, his palms cut up from the broken rocks and cracked earth sliding under them, until he reached the essence of the Moon. He held his bleeding hands into the beams of light cast between the two, palms facing the tiny flower as if yearning to collect up its hope unto his heart, and toward his palms the rays danced, leaving behind only tiny starred scars upon his hands.

The first Moonchild was born through his near death desperation and senses of wonder that such beauty could come from such destruction.

"When again he held his palms above the light in disbelief, he became healed and collected the healing powers of the flower unto his outstretched hands. With that ball of light, just like the one you gathered into your hands earlier tonight, he healed a dying woman. Together, they became Those Who Walked Before Us. They were the first Moon Children and we are of their line.

"They soon revived each dying person left to this world, each different in their culture, no more than a dozen in all, leaving behind a new flower every time, and they formed a village. Animals that still held life, they revived with the powers of the flower. Wilting plants began to bloom.

"Having been raised with the ease of the previous life, going to great storage domes to buy their goods and living in large domes built by others, the people found it difficult to trust in the powers of the Moon for their guidance in starting a new way, but they did trust, and they did survive. That new way has become our way.

They learned to make their own clothes, food, and homes. They traveled on foot, as the first of this world before them. The deadly progress of the past, progress that caused the greed, which had led to the war, was behind them. They chose never to mention it again, and never to remember the old ways of doing things, for the Moon had saved them and the only way for them was the way of the Moon, and it became their substance and sustenance."

She stopped, letting my hand loose from hers to swing back and dangle at my side, as if her words removed all of her strength, as if the past destruction had risen up again and saddened her heart so. "Now, go! Your mother will awaken soon. She will want you there to celebrate with her the Return and the Joining. Come to me as soon as you can for your next lesson," and with that she kissed my forehead and left me standing in the wisp of her sounds in the night.

So many questions filled my thoughts. What big structures? What other ways were there to travel than on foot? What were great stores? I felt I knew the answers in the recesses of my mind, as if I had lived in that other world at some time. I wanted to run after Moon Lady and burst forth all the questions bubbling from my brain, but she had told me to return to my dome, and after all the trouble, I thought I had caused with the Healing, my heart told me to do as she had instructed.

The darkness curled around me, between my thin white ankles and up, and up, but I had spent my life in darkness and my eyes were well adjusted. It was not what I could see on my way home, but what I could hear that left me worried as I entered the rounded hole at the front entrance to our dome.

As I reentered the village through the shrubbery at the edge of the round clearing, after whispering my blessings of thanks to the Moonflower, a heavy step drew my thoughts away into the darkness to my left. Several seconds of stillness produced no more sounds, but still I feared that something, someone, had been watching me from afar. Coyote had played such tricks before, but the heaviness of step had not belonged to him; he would not crunch so many leaves and twigs.

Whatever it had been had not learned the ways of stealth. I continued without another warning from the night and entered the dome to find my mother sitting up, a steaming cup of tea in her slender hands, a smile warming her once pain frozen face.

"Ah, you return, my young wanderer. Herb Lady told me you have been here, by my side for the past night. You've not had much time for games and play with a sick mother, eh? Well, I'm glad to see you have returned. What mischief have you come upon this night while I lay getting well?" she sipped her tea and glanced at me over the top of her earthen bowl.

"Mother," I fell into her lap, my head resting on the blankets covering her knees, my arms encircling her waist. "I'm so glad you're better. I was so worried!"

"Yes, Herb Lady told me she had the Burning talk with you. I'm sorry; I should have been the one, especially after your father's Nothingness. She scared you, with her stories; I can see that now as I look upon you. You have been frightened by the Burning, perhaps wishing for your own Nothingness, but not to fret, Moon

Child, the Joining will go on and we will become a family again. The Herb Lady has healed me." She nodded, her thoughts lost to me.

"But, Mother, no!" I began, a slight tingle from the ball of light lingering on my skin and filling my hands, warming my scars, reminding me of my instruction.

"Go now," she stroked my cheek and then shooed me away to the food on the table brought over by Herb Lady so I would not starve in the night.

I looked back at Mother, but she had already returned to her rest.

I wanted to talk to her.

I wanted to tell her my thoughts about the Joining, even though it wasn't my place to do so. There were many better ones in the village than One Without. He scared me. His son scared me. Or rather, the talk I had heard about them outside my window scared me.

I wanted to tell Mother about the Great War and ask her questions about it. I wondered, while I chewed a bite of cold stew, why I had never heard anything about it before. Nobody in the village ever talked about the past. I grew up believing life had always been this way for us. Perhaps nobody else knew about it either. Moon Lady had said that the first people forgot the old ways. Could it really be true? I had taken everything Moon Lady told me as truth, but this tale of old seemed too unreal to believe. *Tall structures? Other ways of travel? And where would people travel to? And why? Everything they needed was right in their village.* An idea struggled to surface in my memory, but it could not.

I chewed and thought, thought and chewed, until finally I realized I had been sitting at the table the remainder of the night and dawn was upon me.

I put down the window covers, put away the leftover food and crawled into my bed.

That day, dreams of the past filled my sleep. I rode around on a four-legged creature with a long neck. It was very tall, and I laughed as it ran, me on its back. When we stopped at the big dome that housed many other creatures like it, I got into a big moving dome with four, round, black things spinning around on the ground beneath it. It opened in four places, two on each side. A man I did not know sat in front of me on a long, soft thing, and he made the moving dome go. He called himself 'Your Driver.'

I went to see mother, who lived with the One Without in a huge structure and I had to ride in another moving dome with four walls to get to the top, where she lived. This moving dome was very small, and no other was in it but me.

It was dark in her dome when I got there, and she touched the wall and the sun came out! I ducked my eyes into my arms for protection, and she touched the wall again and dimmed the sun! My mother controlled the sun? How strange! I never knew what powers she had before.

I followed Mother into a place where she kept food; it was a whole other dome by itself, and it was a cold dome on one wall and a hot dome on another wall.

A bird chirped and Mother quickly ran to the

hot dome with corners and a door. She called it an oven. She opened it, pulling out some flat cakes that did not look like any I had eaten before. They were very hot, but no fire flamed in the room. I had not seen this power. It scared me.

She brought one of the flat cakes to me; and even though it smelled wonderful, it was made of things I did not know and I would not eat one. Mother frowned and plunked the flat cake back on its flat holder.

All day I dreamed of strange happenings such as these, tossing and turning and groaning so that Mother awakened me with her touch on my forehead twice during the day, believing I too had gotten the sickness. Subconsciously, I believed it was because of One Without that Mother suddenly had these strange powers.

When I woke up that evening, I believed I still dreamed, for the dome had grown! Mother smiled at my surprise. She was a quick builder, the fastest in the village.

That is how she earned the name, Great Builder. Even though she was One Without, many still referred to her as Great Builder, for she had ways with building like no other in the village.

I stared through a new arched door opposite my bedding, eyes wide with admiration.

"Do you like it?" Mother smiled as she stirred a pot over the fire pit.

"You amaze me, Mother! How fast you are at building! I slept only one day!" I stood and stretched, the warmth of the day still lingering in the dome, the sun gone down beyond the mountain to the west. I walked through the opening and turned in a circle from the middle of the dirt floor.

"The walls are still damp, so be careful! Don't touch. One might collapse. Come eat your breakfast while it's hot. You haven't had a hot meal for nights!" I laughed at her joke. One of her walls collapse? That was impossible. That's how great a builder she was!

I sat down at the round table Mother had made from a huge tree trunk that had grown in this very spot. It was dead and petrified by time, its flat surface smoothed down by Mother's talented hands.

For the first time, I wondered at its life before, if it had died during the Great War like so many other things Moon Lady had mentioned. I spooned the hot vegetable stew into my mouth slowly, savoring its delicious flavor, my fingers tracing the rings around the smooth trunk. No meat floated in the wooden bowl, and I longed for some, but it was not Meat Season for the Ones Without.

"So, you feel better?" My concerned look made her smile.

"I am me again. Better, actually. I haven't felt this good since ..." her eyes moved to the bowl before her.

"Father?" I finished for her.

A sad smile slipped over her, but her face soon lit up with joy. "The Joining is in two days!" she answered brightly. "I have much to do before then! I will move our bedding into the new dome when it is dry. I have to make more bowls. I think our store of food will be sufficient, but I must... "

"Won't the One Without have bowls and a food supply?"

"Oh, yes! But with two growing boys in the dome, there is never enough!" she laughed. "Yes, he will bring much with him, as is customary; all will be joined as one. It has been a long time since my first Joining. Your father and I had nothing to join but ourselves. We worked hard to build and fill our needs."

Curiosity took over, and her excitement became contagious. "Who will get the dome of the One Without?"

"Oh, I don't know if the Wise One has decided that, yet. There are two new couples, very young, like your father and I were when we joined, and one of them is in line to receive it," she looked around proudly at our dome. "I'm glad there were no domes available when your father and I joined. It makes a dome so much more pleasurable to live in when you build it yourself."

I was still wary of the boy without purpose who would be joining us, but Mother's joy made me look forward to it. Of course, she worried that we were different as night and day, how true that was, and that we would not bond because of our waking times. There was also his mean streak, but she vowed that a new mother could mend him and help us build our relationship into a real family. Mother swore he would have a name before the first full Moon in our dome.

"So what plans have you this wonderful night?" her eyes squinted with question from below her brow.

"Oh, I don't know, yet. None really, I guess. I'll walk, I suppose, and see what creatures are about," the comforting aroma of my empty bowl still lingered beneath my nose. My stomach rumbled, though I had just eaten. Mother quickly jumped and refilled my bowl with hot vegetables. Carrots, potatoes, corn, beans, and every other wonderful growing plant that stood in the garden of the village lay bathed in little broth before me.

"See, growing boys need to eat! You eat as much as you like," she smiled proudly. We usually did not have leftover stew, or extras. I wondered at this a moment.

"Why so much?" I ventured to ask.

"A celebration! It is one of our last meals together as just us two. Soon, our dome will be alive with the voices of others! We will not often have quiet times for our private talks. Eat!" she coaxed.

We talked more, while the darkness grew through the tiny window on the cooking side and Moon's rays shone down on my sleeping covers. Mother yawned.

"You should sleep now, Mother. You have been very busy today after your illness."

"You are so right my son. Will you take care cleaning? I can hardly keep my eyes open after such a meal and a day."

She moved to her sleeping area and lay down, moments later snoring lightly. I cleaned the bowls in the water bucket, closed up the stew pot, and quietly left the dome for my next lesson. With Mother well, I had some questions to ask Moon Lady of dreams and Great Wars.

8

"Your mother is well, I see," Moon Lady commented after I made my floating journey across the Moonflowers to her dome.

"How did you know?" I fairly exploded in reply. "The crease is gone from your brow; a lightness again fills your heart," she stroked my forehead softly and lifted my smiling eyes to hers.

My face clearly cracked in a huge grin.

"You are ready for the Joining?" a twinge of concern appeared in her eyes.

"Yes! Mother is very excited! I think her joy has caught me. She built a whole other dome onto our small one just today! And we had the best stew and all I wanted!" Moon Lady's delicate arm rested across my shoulders as she led me into her gleaming white dome, nodding and smiling.

"You are happy; that is good! But remember, in your happiness it is easy to forget your responsibilities to the Moon. Keep the secrets. The one who waits to steal the Moon lurks just beyond our joy! If we slip, and the Moon Thief discovers our secrets, our world will change, and our joy will be forever without, as before," she looked sternly at me until I regained a serious composure and listened. "I understand, Moon Lady."

"We have much work to do this night. Some catch up as last night was shortened."

"May I ask you a question?" my dream surfaced again with my curiosity.

"Later. There will be time for questions after the lesson," she led me through the archway of her dome and over to the fire burning brightly at its center. From a tripod stand over the fire, she removed a clay tea pot. She poured two small bowls of the brew within. "Another secret of the Moon," she handed one bowl to me and kept one for herself.

"We will drink this tea and take a journey together into Beyond. When we return, you will tell me everything you see, so you must pay very close attention."

I was scared. I had never been to Beyond and I held the warm bowl with the bitter smelling concoction in my hands, glancing uncertainly from it to Moon Lady, my fear evident in my hesitation. I wasn't even sure what Beyond was.

"Do not be afraid. The Moon will guide us and return us safely. I will not let anything happen to you."

"What will I see? Some of the past? Of the structures and travel? Will I... "

"Questions later, remember? And remember what you see on our journey, for it is very important. Here, hold my hand while we share this tea and we will travel together with hands joined."

I took her delicate hand in my boyish one and lifted the bowl to my mouth with the other. A pungent aroma assaulted my nostrils, yet hidden beneath was the sweet scent of the Moonflowers. I paused, "Is this made from Moonflowers?" my shocked expression released a quiet giggle from somewhere deep within Moon Lady.

"I will show you how it is made when we return, for you will need to make it yourself at times in order to better protect the Moon and its secrets," she lifted her bowl to her lips, a smile still wrinkling her cheeks, and urged me on with her eyes through the steam.

After a first strong taste, the last few swallows became sweet and I swiftly drank the rest without pause. Instantly, my body felt warm, contented and filled with the brilliance, strength and purity of the Moon.

Moonflowers swayed in my thoughts, and I with them, swaying and rocking in gentle breeze beneath the rays of the Moon. My body relaxed, as did my hand in Moon Lady's, and she gripped mine firmer. I felt her touch as if from somewhere in another time and place while my head turned to the journey into Beyond, filling with images of the night.

I walked with the rays of the Moon, following their guidance to a field of Moonflowers where thousands upon thousands of white butterflies danced and played above the beautiful flowers.

A large tree mushroomed out in the center of the flowers, and the butterflies freely fluttered from branch to branch, their beauty and desire drawing me as one of them to the many glowing white blossoms filling the tree branches. From the lower hanging limbs of the large tree, thousands of cocoons hung, delicately wrapped, awaiting their birth into the beauty of Beyond. As I stared with wonder at their glimmering wrappings, one drew my eye. The threads began to break apart, but a fear filled my heart as I watched the birth unfold.

Suddenly I looked around for Moon Lady, who had promised to take the journey with me and there she stood next to me gripping my hand firmly, her eyes glued to me, as mine had been to the cocoon. A layer of comfort took the place of fear, and I returned to the vision of the birth. When the cocoon opened, a strange butterfly appeared first, one of the night, the deepest blue, nearly black in countenance.

But immediately behind it, a gorgeous white butterfly followed, glowing beneath the Moon. I watched as they seemed to play together and suddenly hordes of white butterflies were upon them, covering the two so that all to see was a huge white ball, mimicking the Moon itself.

When the ball dispersed again into the night, no dark butterfly remained, only fields of white.

Presently, another cocoon began its emergence into the moonlight. Another birth of dark and light, but this dark butterfly showed its cunning. It did not play with the white butterfly, its opposite twin.

Instead, the dark one floated away into the night's blackened forest, escaping the wrath of the light, the deadly destruction of the mimicking

Moon, never again to return into my view. Every birth I viewed following offered the same vicious vision of the first barbarian birth, every other dark butterfly disappearing into the ball of light, swallowed up by Moon's army.

Mesmerized by the brightness of the Moonflowers, the rays of the Moon and the Moon dancing butterflies, I did not realize the gentle tug on my hand until the scene before me began to blur to a screen of blinding white followed by the emergence of the Moon Lady and the background of her dome. As my eyes focused, I could see concern in hers, her brow drawn together in anticipation of what I saw. I held onto the long journey in my mind for many moments before speaking, as I knew she would want to hear every detail. I felt tired, as if the journey had taken hours, as if I had watched the butterflies for days, but a glimpse at the Moon beyond the window told me it could not have been but a few minutes, for the Moon had not moved.

Remembering Moon Lady standing next to me in the field prompted a question first from my own lips, still holding a smile of longing for the beauty I had witnessed.

"Didn't you see them? Weren't they beautiful?"

"I saw you. I watched you. I could tell whatever you saw in the Beyond was beautiful, but my purpose in going with you first lay in protecting you and comforting your fears, so all I saw of the journey was you. Tell me now, what did you see that caused you to look just so on your journey?"

I recounted the vision of the Moon, the Moonflowers and the Moon butterflies slowly, my pleasure in reliving the moment evident. Then I told of the tree and the cocoons, but when I recalled the blue-black butterfly emerging, my heart again filled with the fear I felt during the journey and I stopped speaking.

A gentle squeeze of my hand brought me back to present, slightly removing the fear, but when Moon Lady spoke, the fear returned, for in her voice was an urgency that demanded it, "Tell me, now! Do not hold it back for it will fade away. Your fear will overtake the vision and your mind will remove the memory from you in protection. You must not stop!"

My mouth opened slowly, but words tumbled out in a jumble, my fear of the dark butterfly, especially the escaped one, pulling at the words, trying to stop them from being spoken. When I finished, the struggle of the tale left me breathless.

I could not fill my lungs quickly enough with the air I so desperately needed. Each cooling breath expanded them, though, and momentarily my breathing slowed to normal.

"As I feared," Moon Lady unfolded her stiffened legs from their crossed position on the earthen floor and painfully stood, moving to the window and staring out into the moonlit night.

"Feared?" I frowned, remaining seated, trying to regain some energy.

"Yes. Your journey has told me exactly what I suspected. You must be very careful with your knowledge. The Moon Thief is closer than we realize, than I realized!" she whirred around to face me again, the warning of caution aging her face ten more years. "I just don't quite understand it all, the twin birth. There have been no twins born to the villages recently. I do not understand. The opposites, yes, but I am terribly confused. The dark butterfly is a warning of the Moon Thief, though, and we must be very, very careful. If we lose the Moon, again, I'm afraid it will not return and that will mean the end; we shall all p ..." she stopped herself, seeing my brows raise in question, realizing maybe that I was much too young and too new to hear these frightening thoughts.

"Do not fear, Moon Child. Just be cautious. Let me analyze this journey of yours, see if I can determine the true meaning of the One Who Escaped. Be patient and do not worry. You are a powerful Moon servant to have had such a journey! First you heal, and now this, and your lessons are not even complete," she smiled broadly, but it did not hide the distress in her light blue eyes. I realized the seriousness of the matter of the dark butterfly when she gave it its own name.

Nothing in the village received a name until it showed its relativity to the village, and this was one of the most important events in the life of a villager.

With each significant change, a new name was presented to the villager that fit their life at that time. Mine never changed, because other than the one event of the Moonbeams, nothing significant has challenged that event. I realized, given my new insights into my purpose that could not be shared with anyone, that it was likely my name would never change, but I was proud nonetheless, for I did have purpose.

This meant the dark one had purpose to, for now he had a name, more than one for that matter, he was the One Who Escaped and the Moon Thief.

Did that make him more powerful than I? More important? Fearsome?

I wondered at the former name, the one just given tonight, and realized I knew nobody with a similar one.

All questions of the past had left me at the

moment, too, with the future so tormented by the dark. Everything I intended to ask Moon Lady had sunken to the crevices of my mind. The large structures, the means of travel, the strange dream of the day, all had been replaced by a new concern, yet they were not forgotten. They would rise up again without prompting, like the Moon, for in spite of Moon Lady's beliefs in my strength as a Moon Child; I was still left with uncertainty for the future, leaving the past to haunt me for days to come.

9

Moon Lady turned from the window, a smile replacing her wrinkled scowl, "One more lesson, to make up for last night's. You'll enjoy this one, I think!"

I felt a wet caress on my cheek as I sat staring, with furrowed brow, out the window at the Moon and I smiled, knowing who had sneaked up behind me through the open archway. He seemed to make less noise than I at times. I patted the soft hair on top his head, confused about his arrival. He had not been meeting me to walk home with me the last couple of times I came, as I now knew my way. I scratched behind his ears playfully, and, looking up, let my arm drop around his shoulders when Moon Lady began speaking again.

"Welcome, Coyote. It is good to see you well. Moon Child, if you will rise to your feet, we will go out into the moonlight on this pleasant evening, where Coyote will help with your next lesson."

Puzzled, I jumped to my bare feet, glancing from Coyote to Moon Lady. What could Coyote possibly do to help? Has he powers beyond those of the night, his hunting skill and sense of smell?

Curiously, I followed the two out the door, noticing that Coyote's feet padded gently above the Moonflowers, as mine did. There was a light sound, but nothing below for our feet to rest upon. Was Coyote a Moon Child, too? My heart beat with excitement at this conclusion. What else did I not know about my friend, Coyote?

"This, too, you must keep secret from those

you hold dear," Moon Lady glared into my eyes with an urgency I hadn't seen since the first lesson, when I received my stars.

"Of course," I assured her. My head tilted with question. Had I said something to someone? When I had already sworn to secrecy the Moon's powers, why must she remind me?

Her eyes softened as she glimpsed my concern. She looked down at the Moonflowers and back up again, "You will want to share this lesson with those closest to you. Your joy could easily make you forget, but you must remember: *The one who waits to steal the Moon lurks just beyond our joy!*"

"Yes, I remember. You told me before, when I first came tonight. I was confused, because the joining does not make me so happy that I would forget. If anything, it makes me more cautious. I have much to worry about now. Every time I leave the dome, I shall have to be on guard of my actions.

"I think there is nothing that could make me so joyful that I would forget my responsibilities as a Moon Child," I answered solemnly.

"Oh, I trust you completely. However, I know you, too. I know your joy in the Joining really belonged to your mother. Her joy is yours, but when the joy belongs to someone close to you, you have control.

"You are only eleven, soon to be twelve, and this will be the most difficult lesson you will have. When I told you about joy earlier, I was preparing you for this moment, this lesson. It is very, very important that you keep control, and that you always remember. This joy may easily overcome your desire to be responsible. This joy will complicate your thoughts for the next couple of days. You must remember!"

"I don't know if I am strong enough for this lesson, Moon Lady. You scare me with this. Perhaps this lesson should wait until I am stronger?"

"You are strong, Moon Child. The lesson cannot wait. Joy can make you forget your responsibilities to the Moon, but joy will also help you deal with the strenuous tasks ahead. You must be joyful if ever contest comes between you and the One Who Escaped. There are only three who will know this secret, soon two, and it must be kept at all costs."

"The dark butterfly? I don't understand." "In time you will. Be strong. We must hurry now!" That said, Moon Lady spread her hands toward the Moon and gathered its rays unto her fingertips.

Bringing her hands outward gracefully, the rays still glowing from Moon to fingers, she created a giant ball of light, six feet in diameter, in a clearing.

Coyote took his cue and gradually moved toward the ball, his mouth closed, no wag in his tail, as he too understood the seriousness of Moon Lady's words and actions. Into the ball of light he moved, his body quivering with excitement, first the tip of his nose, then his head and shoulders, until all of his body stood consumed by the Moon rays. At the center of the ball, he stood upon his hind legs, his forelegs dangling, and slowly began turning.

Light crackled around him, tiny, blinding, lightning bolts shooting from the coarse hairs upon his body. My light eyes longed to move away from the brightness, as they did from the sun, but I knew I could not stop viewing this important lesson. I squinted through my lashes, protecting my vision, and watched on as he made three turns in the same direction, only his hind legs in motion, and then three turns in the opposite direction.

On conclusion of the third opposite turn, a transformation began. I could not believe this power, this lesson of the Moon. First, the stubby, rounded claws of his forepaws lengthened, until they resembled the fingers of my own hands, but larger, and those outstretched of the Moon Lady. Soon, his paws became hands, and gradually his front legs became arms. I watched in stunned silence as his body transformed to that of human, and the change crept up his neck until all that was left was the long snout that ended in a dripping black nose. Soon, that was gone too, and, but for the long hair on his form, he was human. Moon Lady collapsed with exertion, the giant ball twinkling and dissipating before her. My eyes widened with the darkness, disbelief overtaking them, but I moved quickly to Moon Lady's side, concerned.

"Moon Lady! Are you alright?"

Weakly, she gripped my arm to steady herself.

The coyote-man knelt at her side opposite me, asking the same. Although shocked by his speaking, I was more concerned with the Moon Lady's weakness, and focused only on her exhausted face.

"This power, it is too much for an old lady like me. When you call upon it, you will not collapse, I assure you, Moon Child. Let me rest a moment, among the rays of the Moon and the healing of the Moonflowers. I will be fine. It has been a long time since I used this particular power of the Moon," she breathed with much effort, as if she had sprinted to the village and back. "Do not worry about me, Moon Child," her feeble hand shakily reached the side of my face, and with a tender thrust, she turned my eyes from her.

"While I rest, you should spend this short time with the One Who is Coyote, your father."

My father?

My eyes followed her direction and I looked into the hairy face of the coyote-human kneeling across from me. I sought recognition in the furry face, but the hair hindered my sight. When my eyes rested on his own smiling ones, where no hair concealed, I found him; I found my father in the creases of the smile that adorned the twinkling eyes I focused upon.

10

"My son," we both stood slowly, our eyes locked in joy, and moved around Moon Lady's bent legs. We found each other in a joyful embrace, in which Father lifted me off the ground and swung me about, the hair on his shoulders prickling my bare arms, my heart about to burst with happiness.

"Father," I breathed when he let me down and my toes lifted me up to caress the hair about his brow and his cheek in disbelief.

"It is I, son. Unfortunately, a very hairy me. Moon Lady is getting old," he chuckled, "and has not the strength to complete the transformation," a slap to the arm made him yelp in surprise and we both turned to Moon Lady, who now stood strongly beside us.

"I'll show you old, Grandson!" We laughed among the Moonflowers.

"Oh Father, I cannot wait to tell Mother you are alive! When you disappeared into Nothingness, I thought I lost you forever!"

Moon rays literally danced around and through my body with the joy I felt, but both Moon Lady and my father halted their laughter and viewed me with equal concern and disappointment.

"What is it? What have I done?" I frowned, and then my words returned to me. I looked down into the Moonflowers beneath my feet until a hand upon each shoulder, one delicate, one strong, gently squeezed.

"You mustn't forget," Moon Lady squinted firmly into my eyes. "This joy must only belong to you, son," My father agreed.

"But Mother has been so heavy hearted," my head shook pleadingly.

"But she is now joyful," Moon Lady reminded me of the upcoming Joining.

"And she will be very happy again, soon," my father whispered. The look of caution Moon Lady directed at him was not lost on me. I could wait for explanation.

Some night when Father and I were alone, away from the watchful eye of Moon Lady, I would ask him about that look, about his words.

"Come, we have much to discuss, and celebrate," Moon Lady led us back through the archway of her dome, which seemed to glisten more in the joy I felt at the return of my father.

After a midnight feast and much discussion and laughter, some regarding tricks Father had pulled on me as Coyote, we returned to the waning moonlight.

"Do you have to go?" I hugged Father tightly around the middle, his soft belly fur tickling my pale cheek.

"For now. You will be able to draw the secret power of the Moon to turn me back from time to time, though," he smiled down into my face, then placed a gentle kiss on my forehead. "I will be with you as your friend, Coyote, each night, too."

"Can we meet here tomorrow? Can I change you back again? Maybe I can do it so you won't have all this fur!" We both smiled at Moon Lady, who chuckled lightly behind her hand.

"You must use Moon's powers sparingly, remember? Not for personal pleasures, only for need," Moon Lady reminded me when she looked back at us. "Just like the power to heal," she nodded once.

"Oh, yes. I had forgotten. Sorry," my regret was tangible in the dark night. Would I ever understand the responsibilities I now carried?

"Oh, now, you will have cause to call me back, and it will be you, if Grandmother... I mean, Moon Lady, is correct in her assessment of the future. I will be there to help you and guide, as will she."

"But, Moon Lady isn't it wrong to bring Father

back now? For it has brought me much pleasure, much joy! Isn't that personal pleasure? What will happen?"

"Oh, child, no, it was not just personal pleasure. It was a lesson of the Moon's powers that you needed to learn. I just chose your father as the one to use for the lesson. One night, not long from now, you will practice this power and you will see your father again then. But remember; only you can know of his life and alter life. It is too dangerous for us all if anyone finds out about this power, or about your father," she took my face in both hands and looked deep into my eyes, "very dangerous." Then she spread her fingers again, "Say goodbye for now," she instructed as light collected into her fingertips once more and a large ball of white formed, tiny lights dancing and whirling within.

"I'll see you tomorrow night, son, on four legs."

Father was gone again, but the emptiness I had felt at his loss no longer filled me, because I knew he was still with me, and this time I closed my eyes against the light, a smile filling my face.

I felt a wet tongue on my fingers, and opened my eyes to the sound of Moon Lady's words urging me home before it got too late.

Apparently, it was not as strenuous for her to turn him back, for she was not even winded. I couldn't help myself; as Father and I walked by her, I stopped and hugged her tightly around the shoulders. After all, she was the only person with whom I could share my joy at Father's return, and she was the one who had brought him back to me.

I followed Coyote through the forest with a lighter spirit that night, knowing who he really was now. When we reached the Moonflower, I knelt down and hugged him around the neck, something I had never done before, and in his face, his long furry snout, I could see the smile that had always been there before, but now appeared different to me.

With dawn on the horizon, I scooted into the dome and encircled my freshly awakened mother about the waist before she could get to the arched opening to the outside world. A curious expression filled her face before she scooted around me. Then, I went to lower the hide down over my window so the light would not bother me.

Excitement overtook my thoughts and I could not be still. I went into the new dome, where my bed would soon be. I touched the dry walls about me. I whirled at the center in a dance of happiness.

Mother reentered the dome at that moment, stopping to smile at me from her place at the fire, and then she resumed cooking, her breakfast, and my supper. I had no hunger, though, but did not have the heart to tell her so, for the joy at seeing my father again, as well as Moon Lady's great feast, left me fully satisfied.

"You are happy this morning! Something very good must have happened last night while I slept. Tell me. Another star shower?" Mother squinted a smile at me as I stood stock still in the middle of the floor, my face flushed with energy.

"Uh...no...no, not a star shower," I almost

burst out.

"A new friend perhaps?" her brows raised with interest. She must have noticed the instantaneous widening and dropping of my surprised eyes and misunderstood she had guessed right. "A new friend? Really? Tell me what animal you discovered last night? Or perhaps, just maybe, it was another child, a girl child?" her smile divided her face.

I flushed, and a sense of relief washed over me. "No, mother," I could not lie to her more, and I hoped that she would not ask any more questions so I wouldn't have to lie. Already I had the entire secret of Moon Lady and the powers of the Moonflowers to hide from her. I felt a big wall growing up between us, as if when Mother added on to the dome she sealed me into a small space I could not get out of.

"Not a girl? Then why the pink face? Tell me."

"I... uhm... I just had fun tonight, and, uhm, I have caught your feelings of joy about the Joining, I guess. I mean, I will have a brother, now, although we will be different as night and day," that was mostly the truth.

"Oh, the Joining! Yes, you will have a brother. I think that makes me just as happy as it does you. You are taking this better than I imagined you would." She turned away to start breakfast. I glanced at the back of her, standing at the food box, pulling out the ingredients and setting them on the small trunk table. I wanted to talk to her about Father. It was making me crazy to keep this joy to myself.

Moon Lady had been right. This joy would be difficult to contain.

I knew I shouldn't, but maybe if I were careful... "Mother? Do you still miss Father?"

"Now, there are the feelings I expected from you before the Joining!" a bittersweet smile touched her face. "Of course I miss him, but I know he will never return." She measured out the flour evenly.

"How? How do you know? I mean... is there something inside that tells a person a loved one is gone forever?"

"My, that is a strong question! It is very hard

to explain. I think there is a connection between people, a feeling that tells them when someone is gone. I guess that's why it was very hard for me this past year, for sometimes I felt your father was still alive and near, yet other times I felt he was lost to me forever. That is why I did not choose a new husband during the six moons. You have had some feelings like this?" She stirred the bread mix with her hands, careful not to push the unmixed flour over the sides.

"Yes, I mean, I think I have. Yes, sometimes I know Father is still near, and sometimes I know he isn't."

"Know? You mean feel? Boys and their feelings!"

"But Mother ..." I stopped myself, remembering Moon Lady's and Father's warning. I wasn't supposed to share this joy. I wanted Mother to know so badly that Father was still alive. Would it be wrong if she joined with the One Without while Father was still alive? I would have to save that question for Moon Lady, I suppose. I would pose that question to her tomorrow night.

Although I was about to bust with news, I kept my secrets, for if I told her about Father, then I would have to tell her the rest, too.

"Oh, Moon Child, your father will always be with you, for you are his son. You will always feel him, here," she touched the place of her heart with a floured hand.

"I know."

I was quiet the rest of the time she made breakfast and all through the meal. The talk of father must have weighed on her, too, for she became sullen. When I finished, I lay atop my bedding, sadly wishing all was the way it had been before Father's Nothingness.

11

That day, the dream returned to me again, *the tall structures, the big domes rolling around on black full moons, the small, sweet smelling cakes my mother cooked, but this time, the One Without and his son were there, too. They welcomed me into the dome at the top of the structure, hugging me and offering me different foods I had never eaten before. They wore strange clothes and many sparkling jewels.*

Pictures filled the walls of their structure, some

pictures of me. I had never seen myself except in the lake at night, surrounded by moonlight. As I gazed upon these pictures, I could not focus on my image, for the bright lights blurred and blended against the picture, swallowing my image completely, as if I had no face.

As we sat on the soft chairs and talked, my new brother stuffing his mouth with sweet cakes, my mother constantly getting up and filling the plate, and the One Without telling stories of his travels to many big villages, a knock came at the door. None would get up to open the door, so I did. I could not believe my eyes when I pulled open the door, for a very angry Father stood there before me, and then he shoved passed me into the structure and began searching for Mother, shouting her name over and over.

Without warning, darkness filled the room, the structure, and the outside world. Mother lit a small fire at the point of a stick, but I, being accustomed to darkness, moved to the window, fear filling my heart. Just as I had suspected, there was no Moon in the sky. Where could it be?

It should be full and bright! Was it Moon Thief? Had it happened? Had I been careless and divulged the secrets of the Moon?

I turned from the window, betrayal flooding my eyes; my eyes searched the room for the one who would do this, who would betray my trust, but before I could pinpoint a triumphant glare, a raised eyebrow, or a shift of movement, Mother shook me awake.

"Why do you look at me so? It's time to awaken, Moon Child. Supper will be ready soon, and we have guests coming to join us," She ruffled my hair, but the look of distrust lingered on my face.

Surely Mother would not betray my trust. She knew of the Moonflower just beyond the village, though she may not remember. Cautiously, I arose, dressed and took care of my evening tasks.

Was it possible that Mother was the Moon Thief? Is that why I could not tell her about Father?

Is that why he rushed into the room in my

dream looking for her? Doubt plagued me as I moved around the dome, silencing any conversations I may have had with Mother. She was so busy preparing our meal for our guests that she didn't notice anyway.

I knew who was coming to eat with us, and I began worrying about the son. We had never met.

We never had the chance because I could not go out during the day. I knew how mean he was, though, and I was not looking forward to this encounter. I steeled myself to prepare for any rude remarks he might make.

When the dream finally lifted from my thoughts, I began helping Mother with the order of the table and what little cooking I could do.

"You will meet your brother this evening. Are you excited? I gather you must be nervous, as you haven't spoken much."

What was I to say to that? Not nervous, Mother, more like scared. I couldn't tell her that, not when she was so happy. Lies seemed to be the only conversations I had with her lately. My silence worried her.

"You are okay?" she felt my forehead. "No fever. What is it, Moon Child?"

"I am just nervous. What if they don't like me? What if his son, whom I never met, doesn't like me? I have never been around other children, Mother." That wasn't too big of a lie.

She turned from her stirring over the fire and placed both hands on my shoulders. My head hanging, eyes focused on the dirt floor, she pulled me to her.

"Moon Child, I know it will be difficult for you at first. You are different, special, and other children may not understand. It will take time, but I think you and the son of the One Without will be great friends," her eyes smiled into mine.

"How, Mother? When we can't even play together?"

"We will see. Perhaps he can go out with you one night? He might even like that and start doing it every night! Children are very adventurous!" She turned back to her cooking.

I thought of that, how it might work out, him going with me into the night, running, playing, visiting the Moonflower.

No! That would never do. If he went out with me, I would have to change my routine. I could not visit the flower, play with Coyote-Father, or go to the Moon Lady's dome. *He cannot go out with me*, I thought to myself, *and I most certainly cannot go out with him.*

As night settled in, Mother went around lighting the oil sconces on the walls, providing a very dim light in the room. The table was set for four, the stew boiled over the fire, the tea steamed in the pot.

"Greetings! May we enter?" a man's voice called through the hide door.

Mother gave me an excited look and pulled the door aside to fasten it open. The One Without handed a gift to Mother, and then kissed both of her cheeks in the village custom of greeting. His first look in my direction was exactly what I expected, a look of horror, as if seeing a ghost, but his manners wouldn't allow any rude comments.

I sized him up beneath his stare. He was tall

and slender, his long, stringy dark hair falling to his shoulders as was the custom of One Without. I could see where his son's mean streak came from, too, for all the unspoken words he compiled shown through his eyes. He held great disgust for me and my condition, but he bit his tongue and moved toward me.

"Amazing! You must be Moon Child?" His hand shook as he held it toward me, undoubtedly afraid that I was contagious and he about to change colors. He stared in awe at the transparency of my hand in his deeply tanned one. "Amazing!" he repeated.

Mother felt the tension building in me and ushered in the son, speaking to the One Without to break his concentration and link to my hand. "And who is this?" she placed an arm around the son's shoulder and ushered him into the dome. He flinched away from her touch. One look said it all, but his mouth hadn't realized that.

"Crap, Dad! You didn't tell me we were eating with a ghost? What's wrong with you? I always heard about you from the old people, but man, you are whiter than white! Is that a disease? Is it contagious? I ain't touchin' you! What's wrong with your eyes? I can't even look at them!"

My hand hung in the air, left without shaking.

I looked up at Mother's shocked expression. She looked to the One Without, immediately spurring him to action. He grabbed the boy by his arm and led him outside where any words said were too low for me to hear, and I have super great hearing. A sharp sound of discipline echoed through the darkness into the dome and the two returned, the boy's head hanging, a red whelp glowing on his tanned cheek. I looked at that blonde head with sorrow, for I had never known aggression from my parents. Never once had they been forced to discipline me. When the boy looked back up at me, it was not what I expected, for instead of shame or sorrow at what he had said, he looked angry, as if I had been the one to whip him, or the one who should be whipped.

Mother's embarrassment at this display hurried her to the fire, where she carried the stew to the table and ladled it into the wooden bowls that sat next to a thick slice of crunchy bread.

"Please, sit down. Let's eat while the stew is hot."

I went to my usual spot at the table, but following my eyes there, Mean Child, a name I had been secretly calling him when I thought about him, moved cleverly and quickly to my spot. I did not even protest; I just moved around the table to sit between him and Mother. Mother did not keep her thoughts to herself, though, "That is usually Moon Child's seat for meals, across from me. His generosity at allowing you to sit there is very kind, don't you think?" her brows rose at Mean Child, and he smiled back at her.

"I'm so sorry! You are so beautiful that I could not resist sitting across from you," he charmed.

Mother took the compliment, but she was not one to be charmed by a snake, "Yes, and next meal we share, you may sit even closer to me," she nodded to the seat I now occupied. Mean Child glared at me before picking up his spoon and sucking down his stew and bread.

One Without took pleasure in his food, as did Mother and I. He groaned with each bite, nodding his head while he chewed, but his eyes never left his bowl, as if he could not stand to gaze upon me, the one who sat opposite him. Never once did he look up at me to have conversation.

"This must be the best stew I have eaten in some time," he bowed his head in Mother's direction. "I do not even miss the meat."

"I do," grumbled Mean Child.

His father, who sat next to him and across from me, flung his right hand from the table, instantly smacking the boy with the back of it.

Mother and I fairly jumped from our seats while the boy dropped from his and onto the floor.

The One Without bowed his head, "I apologize. My patience grows thin with his lack of manners. He knows it is not Meat Season. He also knows how delicious this stew is without meat, but I have shown disrespect to you by striking out at him in your home. Perhaps a woman's touch is needed to correct him? I am without any other means by which to make him see. Nothing has worked."

Mean Child rose to the seat again, again flinging evil glares first at his father and then in my direction, but when he looked through his lids at Mother, his expression softened.

I decided right then that I was in for a very tough time with him, and my distrust soon directed itself toward him. My mind instantly determined that he must be the Moon Thief from my dream and not Mother. I ate the rest of my meal in silence, feeling cold, repulsive thoughts from the soon-to-be newcomers to our family. I wished that I were just being overly sensitive, but I knew that was not the case.

I helped Mother clean up after our guests departed. She was tired, but something else lingered in her face, a feeling I was not accustomed to seeing in her eyes.

"I am sorry, Moon Child. I did not wish this. Perhaps this Joining is a mistake. It is my fault for waiting so long to choose, and now my only choice is the wrong one for us," tears fell from her beautiful eyes. I couldn't stand to see her crying again.

It reminded me of the night Father left. If only I could tell her that he was still alive, changed, but alive, yet I could not.

"Do not be sad, Mother. I can handle the son. You have taught me strength. Perhaps you have chosen this way to help him, to give the son your love. He is not well loved by his father, it seems."

She looked through her tears at me, as though revering a Wise One. "How do you think that, when they have treated you so badly? My son is kinder and more forgiving than I. I don't know that I can tolerate their disrespect of you, Moon Child. You did not get that strength from me; it must be from your father. You truly are special and I will always love you. You are right. Maybe I am to help the son, but we could always choose Nothingness over Joining? We could go into Nothingness together?"

As many times as that thought had entered my mind, especially in the past two hours, I wasn't sure it was what I wanted for Mother. I knew what it had meant for Father; I sort of knew what it meant for me, but I did not know what would become of Mother. I pictured her, a hairy human like Father, romping through the night.

Or, perhaps in her Nothingness she would become something incompatible with Father, and then they would still be separated. Besides, it must be Mother's fate to Join the One Without. And, what of Moon Thief?

"What would become of us?" I asked sadly. "Is it not your fate to Join the One Without? I have a mother, but his son does not. His son has a father, but I do not. I am unselfish; he is not, but I can still share my mother with him," I shot an encouraging smile her way, for in my heart I knew this was how it should be, whether we would be happy with the decision or not. Difficult times were ahead, and they would not get better soon.

"You are right, Moon Child. And you are a wonderfully unselfish son whose place could never be filled or taken from my heart. The Joining must continue. We will straighten out that young man if it is the last thing we do," she patted my face gently, and then wiped her tears away.

I wondered if it would be the last thing we did.

I had never before seen violence demonstrated as it was tonight between the One Without and his son. I couldn't tell Mother how afraid I felt about the impatient way in which the One Without struck out at Mean Child.

"How did you get so mature? When did you become so wise?"

I flushed at her comment, "Uhm, I think I'm going to go for a walk, or something. Do you need any more help?" It was late. Could I make it to Moon Lady's and back before dawn? We had much to discuss, and I another lesson to learn.

"No, Moon Child, you go. I am going to sleep. Let the door down on your way out, please."

"Okay, Mother." I waited long enough for her to retire to her bed rolls and watched as she closed her eyes, her breathing shallower, before I left the dome.

13

When I reached the edge of the village, Father stood, tail wagging, ears perked, tongue dripping, waiting to run with me to Moon Lady's dome. I wanted to talk to him so badly, and I knew he would understand, but his advice could only come in the form of coyote speak.

Halfway to Moon Lady's, sensing my troubled heart, he stopped in a clearing enlightened by Moon.

He snipped at the fingers of my left hand and

ran to the center of the clearing. I did not understand what he wanted, for my thoughts were elsewhere, so I started to follow him. He ran back and stopped me, though, not wanting me to stand with him. He hurried back to the center of light and looked back at me, mouth closed, eyes roaming between the Moon and me. I knew then what he wanted. I did not know whether I should perform the task or not. I shook my head at him. Moon Lady had told me not to turn him human unless I needed him. I did need him, but was it for my own personal gain? I stood reasoning until Father yipped in my direction.

"Well, go on. He is waiting," Moon Lady's voice startled me from behind. "You must practice."

"Moon Lady? How? What?" I stammered.

"You must hurry, or you will not have enough moonlight to change him back."

I looked from Moon Lady to Father, and then to Moon high in the night sky.

I closed my eyes and spread my hands, fingertips up, and gathered the Moon's rays to them.

I felt the warmth tingling in my fingers as the rays grew stronger. Without seeing, I directed the Moon rays close to where Father had stood before I closed my eyes. With my hands, I formed a ball of light, six foot in diameter, at the center of the clearing.

I did not see my father walk into it, because my eyes remained closed, not just for concentration, but also for protection. I followed my instincts and somehow knew when he had entered and how long I needed to keep the light circulating in the giant ball.

When I finally dropped my hands to my sides, I first felt weak, but within moments, I became energized again. Still afraid to open my eyes, I stood solid, my heart pumping as fast as if I had sprinted to Moon Lady's dome and back.

"Open your eyes, Moon Child, and witness your strength," my father's voice whispered before me, close enough that his breath lightly blew across my eyelids, down my nose and over my pale cheeks.

Slowly I opened first one eye and then the

next.

Before me stood my father in his human form without one coyote hair upon him. Moon Lady quickly thrust a robe out to him, for he could not wear clothing as a coyote, and he wrapped himself in it, a smile creasing his strong face.

"Father!" I threw my arms about him, as I had the night before, and he hugged me lightly for just a moment before pushing me away.

"There is much to say and little time. Moon Lady, I know, wants to speak with you, and then we can discuss your problem with the Joining."

Moon Lady looked into my face, lit up with excitement, "You are indeed very powerful. You are not even winded, and that is a big task. Now come, sit with me and tell me of your dreams. You have had some, yes? All Moon Protectors do when they first begin learning the Secrets of the Moon."

I followed Moon Lady into the circle of light in the clearing, but I realized, when I remembered my dream, that Father was also involved, and it was right after his arrival to the tall structure that the Moon had disappeared.

"Tell me," Moon Lady instructed as we sat at the center of the clearing. I glanced up at her, then over at my father who appeared just as anxious as she to hear about the dreams I had been having.

Could I trust him? I knew I could trust Moon Lady, but could I trust my father? I could not speak.

"Moon Child, it is very important that you tell me about your dreams, for they help fit together the pieces that will fall into place if Moon Thief should somehow discover the secrets. Perhaps the dreams will tell us who Moon Thief will be and we can stop him before he gains any knowledge of the Moon's secrets."

I looked at Father again, his hairless face smiling back at me patiently, supportive, and I began to speak of my dream from the day before.

"Ahhh... M-hm... yes, I see," Moon Lady added at intervals, nodding her head, while I retold the events of my dream. At the end, the distrust had returned to my eyes, and I couldn't look at

Father sitting at my left side, for fear that he could read my emotions. Since we had become friends, boy and coyote, we had learned to communicate with our eyes, our expressions. Surely, he would know my thoughts. Suddenly, I did not like being a Child of the Moon; a Protector of its Secrets, for the cost was too great. I had always trusted my parents, but now, a confused look spread over me while I watched Moon Lady contemplating my dream.

She understood. She sent Father to the edge of the clearing to fetch the basket I hadn't noticed her carrying.

"You can trust your father, Moon Child... I believe. He has known about the Secrets of the Moon, most of them, for many years. That is why in his Nothingness he became a Child of the Moon, a coyote. Can you trust everyone in your family? No. You must be especially careful around the new members after the Joining. That is what I have understood from your dream. Dreams are another Secret of the Moon. Though the Moon is sleeping while you sleep, the power you gain from the Moon provides your dreams. You are linked to the Moon forever on. The Moon also lets you control your dreams. You may discover many secrets about yourself and those around you while you dream, you have only to stick with the dream and lead the way of it."

Father returned with the basket of food, set it down, and left to get some water from a creek.

After he set the bucket down next to us, he joined us, and there in the light of the glorious, secret-filled Moon we had a picnic, Great Grandmother, Father and me.

I didn't want to return to my dome. The food, though meager as it was, seemed a feast under the circumstances. I wanted to stay with them forever and not return to the ones I couldn't trust. Here I could speak freely and express what troubled me. At home, it was secrets and lies. Somewhere deep inside of me, I felt ashamed for lying to Mother so frequently. I had never lied to her before, and now, it seemed, I lied to her all the time.

With Grandmother and Father, I did not have

to lie. There was no shame. So, after my lesson of dreams, when Moon Lady rose before the falling Moon and suggested I return home, I hesitated. It took great urging from her and Father to move me in the direction of the village. On my way home, I began, with troubled heart, thinking of the lie I would tell Mother upon my return. It tormented me so, that I stumbled over obstacles I had for many nights leaped over easily in the darkness. My again coyote-father yipped with panic at every near tumble I took.

What I hadn't realized, though, on my guilt ridden journey that night was that this lying to my mother was just the beginning of all the lies I would have to tell, and the troubles I had been dealing with were much easier than those coming in the near future.

Even with the toe stubbing and shin bruising journey home, I still made it back earlier than normal and entered the dome silently, for Mother still snored lightly in her new circular room. Moving to my bedroll, I sat cross-legged upon it, pondering the events of the night, what I knew, what I needed to learn. I was so uncertain now of those moving into our dome that fear threatened to tear down the secrecy of my destiny. I listened to the soft snores of Mother, wanting to wake her as I did when I was younger, lay down next to her, and bare to her my troubled heart. She would stroke my hair and listen, finally explaining away my fears.

A tear raced down my pale, Moon glistened cheek, for now, as desperately as I needed Mother's counsel, I could not even trust her enough to tell her my fears. In this, while I was still within the village walls, I was alone. I could not unburden myself to anyone.

So alone in my fear-drenched tears was I that I did not realize the Dawning was upon me and Mother was frowning at me from her neatened bedding.

"Moon Child, why do you cry? What is it? What troubles you?" She moved to sit next to me, but startled, I wiped quickly at my face and stood, moving away from her, thinking hastily of some story to cover my blunder. "Moon Child?"

I turned away from her, moving to the table.

"It's... nothing. I just... one of my friends passed into Nothingness, that's all. I will miss him."

I hoped she was not awake enough yet to hear the hesitation in my story. I hoped this lie was believable and that it was enough to cover the night's events without further explanation.

"Oh, Moon Child, I am so sorry. It is a shame that animals do not live as long as we do and have so much more danger to live with. Let me make you a good meal." Her sympathetic touch on my shoulder almost caused the tears to flow again, but there was no use crying anymore. I was too old for such silliness now. I was too old, and very much alone.

I watched cautiously as she rekindled the flames in the fire and began heating the leftovers from the previous meal. I remembered the disaster of the evening, how the soon-to-be new members of our little family behaved so badly.

"Mother?" thoughts rolled through my mind, and I felt a desperate urge to change their track from the one they previously took, so brazenly I rolled with them.

"Yes?"

"What if ..." The event spurring my question

would hurt her, no doubt, and I stopped for fear of her reaction. She recognized the seriousness of my pause, stopped cooking, and moved to me, lifting my downturned chin with her delicate fingers.

"What if?"

"What if, after they move in, the One Without finds reason to hit me like he hit his son? What if, maybe, he won't need a reason and he just does it?"

"Is that your fear? Oh, Moon Child, that would not happen. You saw the disrespect his son showed. That is what brought about the anger. You have no disrespect and he would not hit you without reason, for that is an act against village laws. He could be severely punished for actions of violence without cause."

"Really?" I brightened.

"Yes."

Moments after she returned to the fire, another question formed in my mind, "Will the One Without receive a new name through the village after the Joining, or will he have to prove himself for a new name? I know his son has to prove himself before he can be named, but what about the One Without?"

"My, Moon Child, you are full of questions this morning. He will have to prove himself after the Joining. That is the way of the village. There have been instances, though, where some major event took place and changed village names just before the Joining. He would keep that name, in that instance."

"I wonder what name he will prove to have."

Will it be Moon Thief?

"I do not know."

Another thought raced through, overtaking the previous ones. So much filled my head right now; I couldn't sleep if I wanted.

"Mother, do you dream often?"

"Oh, my, Moon Child! What a question! Dreams? You know the value of dreams in the village. You have known this since your first dream. Have you been dreaming, again?" she suddenly became worried and rushed to my side, feeling my forehead. She had been this way since her own illness, concerned about my health at all strangeness I exhibited. Finding no temperature, she stared oddly at me. "If you have been dreaming, we need to get Herb Lady over right away. That must not happen!" The urgency of her voice forced me to bite down on a section of lower lip between my teeth.

"I have not been dreaming," I lied.

"Whew," she blew out a relieved breath, "then why do you ask about dreaming and give me such a scare?" I could not answer that. The question had flown into my mind with village laws forgotten. No words came to my mind that fitted together a coherent answer. I opted for the reply of the innocent.

"I just wondered; I mean, why is it so bad to dream?"

"Moon Child, we should not even be speaking of dreaming unless one of us is ill, and I don't really know the answer to that anyway. Dreaming is against village laws and they take it very seriously, curing it very quickly. That is all I know.

"Now, you should come and eat and don't let this subject enter your thoughts again. Today is a very important day for us. You will have to awaken early for the ceremony. As is customary, when the Moon first begins to rise and the sun begins to fall, the Joining will begin. You and I will have to get dressed in our best well before that. Come, eat!"

Another flash, "Mother, how long does the Joining ceremony last?"

"Oh," a tiny glisten returned to her eyes as she began, "the actual Joining doesn't last too long. It's the feast afterward that takes much time."

"Oh," I stirred the broth in my bowl, my wooden spoon spiraled the liquid like a fish surfacing for food, while I gazed into it searching for a solution that did not exist among the vegetables there. "I don't suppose I will have much time to myself, then."

"Oh, you will have time. Not as much as you are used to, but you will have all night after we return to the dome and everyone sleeps. Why do you worry? Do you..."

Just as she began to tease me with what had become her daily idea regarding a 'new friend', the village messenger burst through the open doorway doubled over and panting for breath. His eyes first fell to me with a slight pained look, as though he had just bit into something distasteful, and then they softened in light of my mother and her beauty. It amazed me still, how many of the villagers had never seen me. They knew of me, I was sure, because I had heard other children speaking of my affliction in lowered voices beyond the wall of our dome.

"You have news?" my mother demanded, coaxing his attention and words back to her.

"Yes, Great Builder, One Without has earned a new name before the Joining."

A look of concern crossed over her face now, for fear that the new name of One Without might cause him to refuse her before the Joining. "Well," she began, less enthusiastically than she should have been, "let's hear it. I would know the name to my future husband."

"Coyote Hunter is his new name. This

morning on his rounds, early while most still slept, he smote a coyote trying to sneak in to steal from us, just beyond the village. It hangs now, just outside his dome in honor of his new name, and to scare off others like it."

Mother saw the horror and shock in my eyes as she searched my face for acknowledgment that this was the friend I had spoken of. How often lies must turn to truth after they are spoken! "Thank you, Messenger." She nodded slightly as he turned to leave.

"Was this your friend?" she asked of me.

Tears of fear formed in my eyes and threatened all I kept secret, for now more than ever I wanted to tell her about Father. Father, dead, again? I could not bear the thought. I had to see for myself. "I must go see, Mother!" I started for the door, but her hand held my shoulder firmly.

"You cannot go. The sun is up. You cannot. Later, tonight you may see. So it is not your friend that died last night?"

My thoughts of saving Father overwhelmed me

and I collapsed to the floor with grief.

If only she would let me go, I could save him.

If only I could slip away for a few moments. I could withstand the sun for the life of my father.

Then I remembered. I remembered that if I intended to save my father, the Moon had to be out, and it slept now, as I should be.

It was then the tears flowed. There was nothing I could do; my power came with the Moon. It could only be Father who One Without killed, for he crept around the village this morning with me. He must have gotten caught.

Tears flowed for my father, who would be replaced by the one who killed him in just one short day.

Tears flowed and Mother could not stop them, no matter how much love she poured over me to dampen the wet flames.

15

It was no use. I could not sleep. Father strung up outside the dome of One Without, or Coyote Hunter, and Mother to be joined with him in a short time. I had not closed my red swollen eyes since I lay down on my bed, except when Mother sneaked in to check on me, at which time I feigned sleep.

Most of the day I cried. I cried for the loss of my father, again. I had just found him, could not have even saved him by risking my own life, and could not defy Mother to do so. Chicken, I called myself, guilt overtaking me. I hated myself for being so weak. I hated my stupid affliction to the sun. I hated myself for not doing something, anything that would have made Father proud of me, or Moon Lady.

Moon Lady. That had become another issue. I desperately needed her counsel tonight and would not be able to go because of the Joining. Deep inside, I wished that One With...Coyote Hunter would call off the marriage to my mother.

My hate slowly altered its own direction. The more I thought of Coyote Hunter, the more the hate lifted from me to him. He had killed my father early this morning and now because of his proposal, I could not go and find comfort for my grief.

The more I dwelt on his actions and my dilemmas, the more I hated him, the more the heat rose to my face. Soon hate turned to rage and all I wanted to do was hit him, punch him like he had punched his annoying son, smack him around and show him who was in charge in this house. Images, him rubbing his cheek, him knocked out cold, him lying dead without sign of violence to his body, raced each other through my mind.

Somehow, I knew that I could use Moon's powers to kill someone. It just made sense. If I could use them to save a person's life, surely I could take it away, but how?

And could I really commit such a terrible task? Not, I told myself now, without losing my purity of heart, and thus, my power to channel the Moon.

It wasn't long before Mother shook my shoulder, not realizing that I was already awake.

"Moon Child, wake up. It is time. We must prepare for the Joining. I have the water ready for you. I have already bathed. The women of the village, as is the tradition, have sewn our new clothing. Yours hangs by the doorway. We don't have long before sun down, so be quick about getting ready."

She left the dome so I could bath in private. I dressed sluggishly, using as much time as possible, hoping my delay would postpone the Joining.

Perhaps I could fake illness to stop it? Anything would be better than being joined to the man who killed my father. Perhaps this was the direction my life was to go and when I finally got a chance to speak to Moon Lady, she would tell me the same.

"Moon Child, are you ready? We must go, now."

Mother waited just beyond the dome door. As was custom, when I exited the dome, Mother held out her hand for me to take, the beginning of the ceremony, our white, bead-filled robes flowing, tiny symbols of the joining encircling the hems.

We moved slowly to the center of the village in the dawn of twilight, dark enough to not burn my eyes or skin, but just light enough to begin the ceremony. Many villagers had not seen me in years, as I was night and they were day. We had not passed each other or spoken since that last near fatal experience I had with day light. Many gasped at the sight of me, my skin whiter than a dove, my eyes rimmed with pink, mostly from shed tears, lightest of blues filling them inside, and my hair whitish blonde. They turned away from the near transparency of my skin, their eyes unable to view me as I passed them, for Moon was not fully up yet to make me shine.

When we reached the center of the circle, eyes averted to the ground before us, hands outstretched to join with the new members of the family, Coyote Hunter whispered something to the village Joiner, who in turn asked Mother the question. The two being joined could not speak to each other on the day of ceremony until it was completed. I sensed the question before it was given voice and I knew why he asked. It was his right to make such a request, though very few ever did.

"Coyote Hunter wishes to ask your permission to dismiss the children from the ceremony?" the Joiner bowed her head. Mother was flabbergasted by the question and could not speak. Her anger built quickly. *Perhaps this is the end!* I thought joyously.

Quickly Coyote Hunter leaned to the Joiner's ear again.

"So that our Joining will be as if we are newly joined to each other, a fresh start, a new beginning for us both?"

"But our sons? What of them? They must be joined to us, to each other, so that we may be a whole family!" Blood rose to Mother's face, her anger unleashing upon the Joiner. The realization was too much, for if we two boys were not joined with them tonight it would leave Mother powerless over Mean Child. She would not be able to correctly discipline him, to help him, until we had been joined as a family. She would have no hand in how he was raised, and, on the up side to me, I would not have a father, which was fine with me.

"They can be joined in a renewal ceremony in a few months, after they have gotten to know each other better. My eyes are only for your beauty and for a few months I would have the honor to love only you as if in our youth." Coyote

Hunter flashed Mother an enraptured, captivating smile, which I knew wasn't going to work. She was not one to be charmed. She would stand her ground.

She glanced my way, searching my face for a hint of decision on my part, which was not allowed.

She had to make up her own mind, and standing insecurely as I was before all these people who had not looked upon me for so long, I would not look up and offer any help.

She looked back up at him, her face softening just enough, and smiled faintly, as if giving in, "Okay, we will wait. It will be a trying time for them both, so perhaps that is best. You are dismissed, Moon Child," she kissed the side of my head, letting everyone know how much she loved me, yet slightly embarrassed me.

Being dismissed from the ceremony, I stepped back from the circle nervously, hands folded gently before me, and all eyes upon me. I wasn't sure what it meant to be dismissed until Mother turned to look at me and with a jerk of her head let me know that I was free to leave the ceremony, completely. I hardly contained my joy and ran off to our dome to wait for pitch black so I could disappear into darkness and grieve for my father, whom I only had thoughts for throughout the entire day. As soon as it was dark, I could sneak over, take down the carcass of the animal that once was him, and give him the burial he deserved.

Imagine my surprise, when I returned to our dome to see the body hanging just behind it, at the entrance to the woods. I froze. Tears flowed. Heat filled my cheeks, again. I forced myself to take a step, then another and another until I stood right next to the lifeless form hanging there. I gained my composure and began searching for identifying marks, which was difficult to do without touching the blood-matted fur, so I reached up to within inches of the shoulder.

"What are you doing?" I whirled around. I had never been so scared in my life, even though I immediately recognized the disturbed, angry voice that called out.

"I... I was just looking. I've never seen... I mean..." I stammered with fear and anger.

"Yeah, yeah, just leave it alone! That bag of dead bones belongs to my father and if you touch it, I'll beat you up, got it?" The boy demanded.

My face flushed with rage. Belongs to his father? I couldn't control my mind, my mouth, and I thoughtlessly blurted, "It is my father, this bag of bones, you... you... you..." I realized too late my mistake.

"Your father? How could that be your father, moron? What? You grow hair in the night? Is that why you always leave the village after dark? You one of those half dog people from the scary stories told around the night fires? Gawd, what a freak!"

Then he laughed. It wasn't just a little chuckle at a freak's expense either; it was a full blown roar of laughter that angered me more still. I wanted to ram my head into his pushed out belly while his head was thrown back, but I knew, as weak as I was, that I would be the one coming out worse for the fight than he. Then it struck me. He knew I left the village at night.

When his laughter faded, I forced out the words I needed to ask, "You've seen me leave the village?"

"On, geez, you're stupid. I'm glad we didn't have to go through that Joining. I don't want a stupid, ugly brother. I always see you leave. Who wouldn't? It's not like you're sneaky about it or anything. You glow under the Moon like a torch!

"Besides, you're like a bear clomping through the brush. Are you sure your father's not a bear?" More uncontrollable laughter followed this question.

I must be more careful, I thought, looking down at the ground so as not to make eye contact and give myself away. I hoped maybe if I just stared at the ground, he would leave me be, just walk away laughing and leave me alone for the rest of the night. Instead, in the waning twilight, he picked up some rocks and threw them in my direction, forcing me backward, while chanting, "Freak, freak, freak," repeatedly until I stood well away from the dome in the shade of the forest where he could not see me.

"Ah, you're just some weirdo freak. I don't have time for you. I'm going back to the feast. Dork!" he yelled as he retreated to the safety of the inner circle of the village.

I stood in the cool darkness of the forest staring at the carcass hanging behind our dome. I would have to wait until he was asleep to take it down. I would have to wait until they all slept. So, what to do now? I did not want to go back to the village circle and celebrate the Joining. I was not hungry, had not been so since I heard the news of the coyote.

Besides, the people all felt as my new brother did. I was a freak to them, a large white freak that didn't belong. Tears burned in my eyes, until the slightest touch, smooth and moist, on the dangling fingers of my right hand stopped them. Could it be?

I looked, and there, standing next to me, tail wagging, was the coyote who was my father. There he was, shooting up to me a look of concern.

There he was; he was not dead.

My hand bounced when his nose bumped it, as if telling me we had to go, so I turned and we left the edge of the forest surrounding the village, seeking deeper darkness and the only one I knew who could truly understand how I felt. My father was alive after all, but I was still a freak unworthy of Joining.

I ran faster and surer than I ever had. I knew the path well now and did not stumble. Father ran next to me, his four legs keeping easy stride to my two, a canine smile filling his furry face, his tongue lolling with the race. I did not stop to rest, nor did I stop when I reached the Moonflowers but flew over the top of them as if on a sheet of ice.

Out of breath, I reached the white dome in the center of the shining flowers and placed my hand on the side while catching my breath. Sharp edges pierced my hand, and for the first time I ran my hand over the dome. It was unlike any builder's material used in the village, unlike the mud and clay and wood pieces. It shone beneath my fingers in the light of the Moon like tiny gems.

"Quartz," a soft voice answered the unasked question.

I looked again, running my hand over the rough surface. "All of it?"

I couldn't believe I had never before noticed, never inquired about this wonderfully white, shining dome before.

"Did you build this all by yourself?" I turned to look into the eyes so much like mine.

"Oh, no, this dome has been here for many centuries. It belonged to the first Moon Woman. I'm not certain of its entire history, how or who built it. For all my knowledge, I would prefer to believe Moon itself was the builder. It is beautiful, though, and I have very much enjoyed living in it, as I am sure you will, too."

A thought occurred to me at that moment, not a new thought, but one that I had set aside until this moment, with the drama of the past few hours.

"I will live in this dome?"

"Certainly, when you are ready. Which could be very soon. You are learning quickly and are much more powerful than I had imagined you would be. We have had cause to skip some minor lessons, you are so quick to learn."

"Moon Lady, Grandmother," I appealed to her nurturing instead of her instructional side, "is it possible that I might be able to live here sooner, perhaps as soon as tomorrow?" The pain in my voice evident, she looked upon me with a deep concern and grandmotherly expression, weighing the possibility.

"Something has happened? Is it the Joining? I could not make it to the Joining. It was too far a walk given my energy today. What is it, Moon Child? What happened? Tell me," she placed her delicate hand on my shoulder and I peered up into her eyes pleadingly, hot tears forming. She drew me to her and held me tightly, allowing the pain and anger of the last few hours to dampen her glistening white gown, and then she held me at the shoulders and drew back to look at my tear stained face, rivulets of dirt washed clean by the flood of emotion. "Tell me."

I recounted the frustration first of Coyote Hunter and his new name, and how I thought Father had died, again. Next, the embarrassment and humiliation of the Joining, the people staring, tumbled forth in a jumble of breathless words.

"I see," Moon Lady responded quietly. "Well, I believe this to be a good prelude to your next lesson, and since you are here unexpectedly, we may as well do it tonight," she led me into the dome and to the fire burning at its center, where she sat on one side and I faced her from the other. The reddish, orange glow of the flames flickered off her face as I sat in anticipation of my next lesson. Her solemn look as she stared into the fire sent shivers of fear down my spine, though, making me realize that this lesson must be of the utmost importance.

"I need to share with you a story of the past. It is not a legend or tall tale passed down through the ages by the elders of the villages, but a truth, a truth about evil in its worst form, its worst sense. Its origin is as old as time as we know it, as old as the Moon People. The truth holds special meaning for me, however, because of my direct link personally to the evil," she paused, looking down at her once calm hands now wringing with the difficulty of the truth she was about to share.

"You remember our conversation about the butterflies? The dark butterfly in particular?" I nodded. "The Moon Thief is as old as the Moon People, the protectors. After the Great War and the Moon's help and guidance, one in particular withdrew himself from the people. He knew and remembered the old ways of doing things from the past, the easier life of the prosperous. That is what he wanted, the easy ways back again. He did not like to walk everywhere he went; he did not like to hunt; he wanted nothing to do with a difficult lifestyle. He wanted the old ways. He wanted prosperity at the expense of the Moon, the world. But it was our promise to Moon, who so generously saved our lives, healing the people, plants and animals left on the earth after the devastation, that we would live simply, taking only what was needed to survive, and at all costs protecting what Moon offered us.

"The Dark One could not vow to that, though. He obsessed over the old ways, always inventing things he believed would improve our way of life. He simply would not follow the rules of the villages, so, they sent him to Nothingness," she sighed, the hardest part of the story still yet to come. I felt her insecurity, then, as tangible as a thick mist in the night.

"But he came back," I guessed.

She nodded again, "Yes, he came back, as if from the dead, and with him came disaster in its worst form, for to obtain what he wanted, he stole the power. One tiny Moonflower was all it took to bring the wrath of Moon down upon the villagers, one tiny flower. Moon hid for many nights, not giving light, not giving life, not healing the sick. It was a bad time for all, and the only way to fix it was to lock away the Dark One forever in his own blackened dome, sealed shut up inside, like an animal in a trap, and so they did. They caught him in a trap one night while he tried to harvest the Power of the Moon and use it to gain materials he needed to build a city. He tried to use Moon's powers against them unsuccessfully.

"They trapped him and held him until they had the dome almost complete, all but one small hole in which to push him through and quickly seal off. There he would stay until he faded away."

"Could he not use the powers to get out?" I knew the powers were surely capable of that at least.

"Oh, no, to do so, he would have had to have access to Moon's light, and they left no windows in the tough onyx dome they had built to maintain him. Basically, he was entombed alive."

"Then, why do we have to worry about a Moon Thief now?"

"Remember, he once was a member of the village, and he had a wife. Before he was sent to Nothingness, he and his wife were expecting a child. After they sealed him in his dome of darkness, she gave birth. The village leaders wanted to send away the woman and child, but she had always been a dedicated village member, and she had great value, for she was an Herb Lady. She vowed that her child would remember her new husband as his father, but the child began to dream, and as you know, dreams were not allowed in village law. A child who dreams is treated with special herbs, and if that does not work, they are sent to the dream dome for such a time as to eliminate their dreams. The child could not be treated, either by herbs or the dream dome. The last resort was Nothingness, and the mother could not let that happen, so she allowed the dreams and kept them secret, as you must. The villagers believed the child cured, but he was not.

"His dreams filled his mind day and night, dreams of his real father locked away in the darkness of his own making, of a past joined to a future with tall domes and progress. The mother kept his secrets until her death, at which time he left the village with his wife, not to return until much later after he had devised his plan. His wife was my ancestor, our ancestor, the mother of the Moon Protectors," she paused and sighed a deep breath filled with emotion of the ages.

"She was evil?" Puzzlement filled my words.

"Moons, no, but he was! The two bore twins, a boy and a girl. The girl unnaturally light skinned, sensitive to the sun, as you and I, a disgrace to her father, who looked upon her as a freak of nature," her choice of words stung me and I immediately felt kindred to the girl. "The girl was to me, as I am to you.

"She lived in darkness, her father having nothing to do with her, with only her mother's love to guide her. Soon her mother realized that the girl was special, had special powers beyond those she had encountered before. She kept them from her husband, but she could not keep them from the brother, who was the girl's complete opposite, yet of her own spirit and flesh.

"As the twins grew older, the boy desired his sister's powers, and he spent much time with his father, plotting and planting seeds for a convenient and lazy future, seeds of evil against Moon, seeds to steal its powers. When the twins became of age, a little older than you, and the sister came into her full Protection Powers, the boy tried to kill her and take away that which Moon had given her. The mother came upon the struggle and stopped her son, leaving a very nasty scar on his right cheek, at which time she returned to the village and begged forgiveness and protection for herself and her very powerful daughter.

"The daughter dreamed each night, and her dreams became stronger and more vivid than any normal dream of power. Moon taught her through her dreams how to use its powers for the benefit of all, and also to show her that she was still in danger. Moon wanted her to leave the village, go into Nothingness, to protect her, so that she in turn could protect Moon. Through dreams she was told not to confide her abilities to anyone, as the more people who knew of her power, the more she would become endangered because of those powers.

"One dream led her here, to this quartz dome, this field of Moonflowers, where she lived forever, alone to her old age, but not before she had passed on the power. When the time came, Moon sent her another just like her to train in its ways of power, one light skinned of the night, who also trained another, and so on, until we come to now, you and me."

"What of her brother, the evil one?" I asked hesitantly, already suspecting her answer.

"Oh, he continued on, too, training and instilling in his children and grandchildren the ways of evil, the ways of progress, the ways which had eventually led to the Great War of the past and the many changes the world faced afterward. His line continues, in hiding and waiting, to steal the powers of the Moon for their benefit of rebuilding a careless, lazy, and greedy world of followers. Moon Thief needs our powers to be successful in his projects. So we must hide, remain secret, and protect with all our being Moon knowledge, all so the world, the people, will continue to thrive and grow. The end of the Moon means the end of all things."

I recounted her lesson, concerned about the dreams of progress the evil ones dreamed about. "I have dreamed of progress, I guess, the tall structures, the strange travel, have I not?"

"Sadly, yes, and you must be careful that your dreams do not tempt you to old ways."

"But, if I dream progress, then I must be evil, too," my brows furrowed with fear.

"And that, Moon Child, is where my shame enters this recount of the past. Every other generation of evil bore twins, but not every generation bore a Moon white twin. The next set of twins born to evil was two boys, one of which split from the commune of evil and found his way to Moon's village. Upon proving himself, the village allowed him to stay. He did not harbor evil ways or thoughts, in fact, he was against them, but the dreams still came to him. Knowing the village laws on dreams, he kept them to himself, trying desperately to block them out, to forget them. He was your grandfather," she let that sink in, and it didn't take me long to figure it out.

"If he was my grandfather, then I should be..." I stared hard at her.

"Yes, you should be a twin, and you were, before you were born. I knew before your mother announced her joy with you, through my dreams, that she would have two sons, one light, and one dark, hence the cocoons and butterflies of your vision. I knew at that time that I would have to tell you the entire story. Moon also showed me that this had been the Dark One's plan all along, to reenter the village and grow his ranks among the more powerful. Moon led me to your father as the one who dreams of progress, although he always seemed good; your mother as one who is of the light, from my line. I knew from my dreams that the dark twin they bore would kill the twin of light. You would have died the night before your twelfth year. That is why your father was sent to Nothingness. You were coming into your full powers and I could not risk that he take them from you, even though he may not be the one who will," she smiled apologetically at the canine sitting just inside the doorway.

"Moon showed me what I had to do to stop the killing of the Light One, but I acted too quickly in my desire to fulfill my duty to Moon and protect its secrets," a melancholy expression filled her features, her wrinkles more prominent than before, as shadowy flames danced across her face.

"What happened to my twin, Grandmother?"

Her hesitant answer came quietly, shame filling her pained eyes, "I killed him before he was born, before you were born."

"You killed my brother?" I did not know how to feel, what to feel, the emotions rolled around in my heart without order, without guidance. I had had a brother, albeit evil, I had had a true brother, one who would eventually kill me and steal the powers of the Moon, mislead my father, and only to repeat a tragic history. My immediate anger towards her dissolved into a sense of duty to our purpose, but still, I would have had a true, bloodborne brother.

"I know you are disappointed in me, but you must understand, that to protect the secrets you may have to perform unthinkable acts yourself. I am not proud of the act I committed, especially not of the overwhelming need with which I acted too soon upon it, because that rush to fulfill it created a problem," she said softly.

"The dreams?"

"Yes, the dreams. In my desperation to succeed, to save you, I gave your mother the herb sent from the Moon, which would steal the life of the dark one within her, and then I waited.

"During the next few months, I had horrible dreams, dreams that warned of my hurried actions. I waited, hoping the dreams were born of guilt, for I had never taken another life in all my years. When the time finally came for your birth,

I assisted Herb Lady in delivering you and your brother, but I was horrified by the result. You, and only you, were the baby to come to your mother that day. My dreams had been correct. In my rush to serve Moon, I had realized too late that you had absorbed your twin before birth and now carried the split of light and dark within."

My jaw hung open. Did I really hear what she had just told me, or had I drifted to sleep and dreamed this craziness. I could not speak for a long time; only stare into the blue eyes, so much like my own, which held many more questions. "I... am... evil? Dark? That is why I dream of the past mixed with the future?"

"That is why you dream those dreams. You must be very careful to not be lured into the temptation of mixing past and future for convenience."

"But if I am evil, the dark one, too, then why must we worry about a Moon Thief? You took care of him. He is gone, right? And I can control him? Right?"

"Your brother was just one in a line of many.

Evil never stops, progress always wants discovery, life always wants change, but Moon forbids it. The connection of light and dark within you gives you powers you will need now. You are more in tune to the dark than any other Moon Child of the past; therefore, you should easily catch and contain him, or her, as the case may be."

"So, you don't know who the Dark One is, then?"

"No, but your dreams will tell you who it is when you need that information. Moon will always guide you if you do not abandon its ways and become greedy. *Seek only to use the powers of the Moon when you absolutely need them.* Remember that, and also that it could be someone close to you."

Close to me? I am closer to me than anyone, and I am split, "What happens if I fail? What happens if I can't stay good, Moon Lady?" The panic in my voice made my words thick and difficult to speak.

She looked down into the dancing flames that soon reflected in her eyes as she peered sadly into mine, "Darkness. Darkness will rule the world, for the Moon will forsake us and all will pass. There will be no Light of Life. Make no mistake, either. The Moon Thief will try to sway you to evil, and this Moon Thief, given my mistake, will be the most powerful of all so far, hence your lesson for tonight, and probably the most difficult, for you must split the power, two lessons in one."

She rose to her feet without support of her hands, more gracefully than ever I have seen her move, her long white gown flowing about her as she turned toward the door, her grayish white hair waving down her back like a foamy ocean. I moved quickly to follow her, feeling as though I had aged ten years with tonight's lesson already. I suppose if the age of my brother were added to mine, I would be as old as I now felt.

I followed Moon Lady to the clearing we sometimes used for lessons, off the Moonflowers I stepped, through the dark trees--a bridge between the two meadows--and into a sea of flowing grasses driven by the gentle night breeze. The motion made me think of the Joining celebration. There would be dancing, now, probably. Dancing that Mother had excluded me from with her dismissal, which I had gladly taken. I hadn't thought of the celebration all through Moon Lady's lesson, but now it filled my mind, as did the question I had asked her earlier about not returning to Mother.

She stopped several feet from the center of the circular meadow, "Come," she waved her hand to me in an urgent manner, for I had lagged behind with my thoughts.

"To split Moon's powers, you must be thinking of the two things that you will do with it. The only time you will need to split them is to catch Moon Thief. You are the only one who has the power within you to do this. The last time it was done, it took a whole village."

"But the last time, his line continued on. What is the point of catching him if more follow?"

"Moon Child, the point is life. In the dark, there is one more powerful, always, just as you are the most powerful in the light. There may be one like me, but she is weak and getting old like me, too. It is the younger one, the most powerful one that you must catch. That is why Moon called upon you; I called upon you, at such a young age.

"You will catch this Moon Thief before the line can be passed, and if the line has already passed, then you must stop the line, too. All of them, the ones that follow, must be locked away in the black dome, which means you must lead them here, keep them controlled, and build the dome, all using Moon's powers and guidance, splitting the power."

I looked into the darkness of the meadow. Moon's light seemed to fill the entire green orb with light, yet not beyond, leaving the forest in darkness.

I peered up at the Moon, unsure if I were ready at all for this great task placed upon me, and while I stared up at the Moon, I thought I saw the faint outline of a face which now smiled assurance down at me.

"Are you ready?" Moon Lady asked quietly.

"If I build the dome now, will I be able to remove it?"

"Oh, certainly. You will need great concentration, too. Focus on the tasks that need accomplished, then concentrate on Moon's light. Reach out for it as you never have before. Coyote will play the part of Moon Thief so that you will have a target with which to practice, won't you?"

Father-Coyote whimpered at the chore given him and slowly backed away from me. I could tell he was not completely convinced that this was a part that he wanted to play for the cause. I understood his panic, for he was of the dark, as I, and the chance that he really was the one to try to steal the powers still stood before us, a great wall of distrust, so his role in this lesson could very well be a foretelling of his future.

I looked into his saddened brown eyes. Could I really trust him? I glanced over at Moon Lady. If I were of the light and the dark, could I really trust her now? My confusion coursed through me with the blood that heated my body in the brisk night air.

Again, I searched Moon for some answers, for someone to trust, but this time, even the light face within no longer looked back, leaving me completely alone.

"Are you ready?" Moon Lady repeated gently.

"Yes, I guess I am, even though I am uncertain still what I am to do." I looked at Father in his canine form, no more than twenty feet away, no enthusiasm for what he was about to go through.

"You must contain him with Moon's power from one hand and build the dark dome with the other. Before the dome is complete, you must coax him with your powers into the dome and then seal it entirely."

"You're sure I can undo it?"

"You will have to in order to rebuild it later. Only one other such dome has been built in the past and it since has been removed from this very spot in order that another could be built for the newest and most powerful Dark One."

I nodded, picturing what the remains of that Dark One must have looked like after so long trapped in the dome.

With my left hand, I reached out to Father sitting off center of the meadow.

With my right hand, I reached toward the center of the meadow, visualizing the dark dome. I felt Moon's rays warming the stars of my palms, gathering the powers within my hands as I concentrated on the two separate tasks.

After what seemed like hours, beams of light shot out of my fingertips, enclosing Father in a circle of light so bright I had to close my light eyes again and see with my mind. Rays of light from my right hand shot toward the center of the meadow, forming a half circle there. Beginning with the bottom of the dome, in my mind's eye, I built a circular floor, so Moon Thief could not dig his way out. After the floor, the spherical wall around the floor slowly grew up, but I was careful to leave a hole in which to move Father through.

As the dark dome stood almost complete, save

for the hole, I pictured Father moving toward it and through the hole, guided by the beams of my hand, after which I saw the hole seal up; no opening remained.

When I felt the warmth of the rays leave my hands, I opened my eyes again. There in the center of the meadow stood the dark dome. No coyote stood beside it. I must have sealed him in. *And what if this was a rehearsal of what is to come?*

As if in a dream, I moved toward the dome, sliding my hand around its smooth, cold surface while I walked its circumference. It felt like winter, like the water that freezes in the coldest months, like the ice that falls from the sky. No sound came from within, though just before I had sealed it, a desperate howl sounded through the night air. I wondered if the cold and silence were inside, too.

"You must hurry and undo it, or your father will suffocate!" Moon Lady commanded.

In all my curiosity, I hadn't thought of the lack of oxygen within the dome, for there were no openings. Essentially, it was a tomb to the tenant enclosed within its half circle. I moved away and stood again next to Moon Lady, still in awe of my creation.

I wasn't sure how, but following my instincts, I spread my hands outward so it appeared I held the dome between them. Moonbeams zipped toward the star patterns on my palms and zapped out my fingertips once again, to encase the black dome. My eyes closed, I envisioned the dome melting away into the shimmering bright light around it. When the beams ceased, I opened my eyes, and there, where the dome had stood, only Father in his canine form remained, happy once again to be free and trusted for now.

"Amazing!" Moon Lady breathed. "How do you feel? Are you tired? You should sit down," she instructed, her hand pushing gently on my shoulder.

Surprisingly, I didn't feel tired at all. Just the opposite, I felt energized, invigorated! A thrill ran through me after having completed my task so perfectly, remnants of the power coursing through me, I supposed. I felt my pale face glowing with joy.

"No, I feel great!" I almost sang, shrugging her hand away.

"You hold within a very strong power, Moon Child. I have never witnessed or heard of stronger."

Father yipped and bounded toward us, tail wagging. He howled his thanks to Moon in coyote song, and then he sat at my feet as awestruck as Moon Lady.

Something welled inside me with the power I had accumulated. I had never before had reason to feel pride in myself, but now... now I felt as though nothing could stop me. I walked on air the rest of the night, in Moon's light. I believed that I could stop Moon Thief when the time came and that all would be well. Moon Lady quickly noticed my mood, though, and resumed her teacher-like manner.

18

"You mustn't let the power go to your mind. You are happy, and well you should be, but do not believe for one second that Moon Thief is like Coyote. Moon Thief will fight you. It will not be such an easy task when you are facing the real Dark One, especially if there is more than one to contain. You have amazing powers, but you need to keep your focus at all times in order to keep those powers."

"Yes, Moon Lady," I solemnly answered,

knowing that it had been wrong to lose my control in the pride I felt and if the same happened during my battle with Moon Thief, he would surely win.

The three of us walked back to the white dome in silence, Moon Lady and Coyote still in awe of my powers, Moon's powers, and I, I was rehashing all of the night's events and wondering how the Catching would really play out when the time came.

"Must I return to the village, Moon Lady?" I found the time to leave upon me, but I really did not want to return home.

"I'm afraid so, Moon Child, but I feel it will only be a while longer before you will return to this dome forever," her sympathy for my plight of returning to the village did not ease my desire to stay.

"Is it really necessary?"

"Yes, you must return so that you can determine who Moon Thief is and capture him or her. If you are here with me, we may never figure out who it is," she walked me to the edge of the

Moonflowers. "Be very careful, though, that you do not divulge the Secrets of the Moon to any other. If you do so before you capture Moon Thief, we could lose everything."

"Yes, Moon Lady, I will be careful," I agreed sadly as I worked my way into the forest.

I reached the edge of the village well before dawn, so I sat next to my old friend, the single Moonflower, and recounted all I had learned so far.

If I were to come against Moon Thief tomorrow, had I learned enough to win over him? What of the evil within me? I did not feel evil. I did not know. Would I have help? I did not know that either. I stroked the petals of the Moonflower gently as I used to, and in its state of affection, it comforted me, so I stayed.

"What are you doing out here? Where have you been all night? The coyote has been stolen! Did you take it?" the rough voice made me jump.

I moved to hide the Moonflower from his vision, but it was too late. *If I had not sat so long this would not have happened,* I scolded myself.

"What's that behind you? Is that some kind of stone? Get out of the way!"

I stood my ground even when Mean Child shoved me and tried to pass. I shoved him back and began yelling to cause distraction, and hopefully, to get Mother's attention.

As predicted, she came running at the sound of my voice, at which time she spied Mean Child and me rolling around on the dusty earth in a heated battle to gain the upper position.

I could not believe that I could even gain the upper hand in this; he carried much more size than I did. I had not wrestled with anyone since well before Father changed, and that only in play, yet my weak arms, wiry frame, seemed to toss Mean Child as if he was no bigger than I was.

Apparently, Mother also had believed that I did not have the strength or the means in me to fight, because her look of approval as she dragged me off Mean Child rivaled the look of disappointment she gave him. She moved toward him in rebuke.

"But, I was just trying to pick you a flower!" he sniveled.

The sun barely peeked over the horizon and my eyes already began to burn, but I could not leave the Moonflower to Mean Child's mercy.

"What flower? There are no flowers here," Mother's hand swept the area about us. "You are just a fighter, stirring up trouble with others all the time! You should not even be out at this time of the morning!"

Both Mean Child and I turned to look where once the Moonflower gleamed brightly in the night. It was gone! Of course, I knew why.

"It's gone! It was right there! What did you do with it? Where is it?" he yelled at me, circling behind me to see if I had picked it and held it in my hand. "You took it just like you took the coyote from the pole!"

Mother had been shaking her head in his direction, but she now fixed me with her eyes, "Is this true?" she asked without conviction.

She thought she knew me too well to believe I had done something crazy like that, but she didn't know me, not really. No matter, I had not taken it, but instead felt the guilt of all the untruths I had told her recently.

"No. I just wanted to see it earlier, touch it. Now it's missing." Mother remembered my heartbreak of the previous day and glanced quickly at the ground and back at me questioningly. "I didn't take it, Mother. It wasn't mine to take, just like the flower wasn't yours to take!" I sneered at Mean Child.

"It wasn't yours, either, but you took it anyway!"

I shook my head, "I didn't take it; I told you. I took neither of them. I have to go in now," I wiped at my burning, watering eyes and shaded them as I walked toward our dome, the sun peeking out behind the trees, beginning to bite at my delicate skin, making my eyes water more.

"That's right, you crybaby, cry, cry for every lie!"

A loud crack split the silent morning. I couldn't believe my ears! Even though Mean Child and I had not been joined with them,

Mother was bold enough to take her rightful place as disciplinarian of Mean Child, and did she ever discipline him! This could cause her some real problems later, I thought as I entered the archway of our dome just in time to see the back of a hand coming straight at my nose.

I awoke to whispered arguing, my nose so swollen I could barely see around it.

"I told you they should have been joined last night! Look what you have caused!" Mother firmly whispered as the bone she used to stir the sweet cake batter clattered around the sides of the wooden bowl.

"I really thought they could wait. I'm sorry," squinting through my eyelashes I could just see Coyote Hunter raising his arm to Mother's shoulder.

She could throw him out of the dome for good. It

was her right. He knew that, too. *Clever charmer.* I looked around the room. Next to the opening between the two domes, Mean Child sat, leaning into the wall, staring at me, a wish of death in his eyes.

"This is all your fault," he hissed quietly, holding a cloth to his nose. Apparently, he had received the same as I had when he entered the dome.

"And another thing," Mother continued, "Never, ever touch my son again. I told you he could not go out during the day; he went out at night, but you didn't listen. One night we have spent together and already you don't listen to me! I will never touch your son again, and you will never touch mine!" she growled in his direction. "They shall never be joined! I have a good mind to release you from our joining, for as much as you love violence! I will see to it that those two boys will forever stay apart!"

"Forgive me, my love," he took her hand in his and kissed her palm. She jerked it away. I had never seen Mother so angry, her anger thick and suffocating in the dome. I almost felt sorry for Coyote Hunter. I sat up, a pain shooting through my neck, over the top of my head and into my swollen nose.

"You know, I'm not one for anger, but at this time I

am too angry to discuss this. I need some quiet time to think about whether this was a mistake or not. Not that I had any choice, really. Has the young couple moved into your dome, yet?"

This shocked Coyote Hunter so that his face paled and his eyes widened.

"No," he croaked uncertainty. It was a terrible shame to be removed from the dome of your wife at any measure, but after one night? He would be the cause of laughter throughout the village! Soon, his face reddened with rage. A glance at Mean Child's smug face as he stared at Mother told me what would happen next if I didn't intervene, so weakly I called out, "Mother!"

She came running to my side, her hands gliding over my face, cooing and cawing over my swollen nose. She replaced the poultice.

"Are you hungry? The cakes are cooking."

The scent of her sweet cakes drifted through the dome. They were the best ever. "I could eat, I think."

"Let me help you up. Careful, you may still be dizzy." She was right. I stumbled three times on our way to the fire where Mother looked across the flames at Coyote Hunter and calmly stated, "Please take your son and go back to your old dome for a day so that I may have time to think about how best to handle this.

20

Truthfully, Mother could not bring this incident up before the village, as she had struck Mean Child first, but she did have the right to remove Coyote Hunter from her dome and request quiet time without question.

"Fine," Coyote Hunter answered sharply, "But you really shouldn't baby the boy like that. How do you expect him to grow into a man?" and with that he stomped out of the dome, Mean Child on his heels, not sparing a hateful glance in my direction.

As he passed, his greedy hand reached for a cake and ripped it from the top of the table.

Mother shook her head, putting down some sweet cakes for me. I pulled a piece free, placed it in my mouth and tried to chew, but the pain it brought to my nose dulled my hunger. Mother suggested that I let the cake dissolve on my tongue and then swallow.

"You have to eat to keep up your strength, even though you seem to have plenty more than I imagined!"

So I did, I nodded. She winked at me regarding the fight and we laughed, causing me more pain. When I finished my meal, she changed the poultice and gave me some herb tea to dull the pain so I could sleep. She covered my small window, pulled the cover on the door and left the dome, no doubt to speak of her problem with the Wise One.

I did not know what would happen, what would become of Mother and me if she removed the joining ties, but I felt, now more than ever,

Nothingness a better choice than Coyote Hunter and Mean Child.

Afraid to sleep alone in our dome, I pondered on our recent fighting. Mother and Father never fought while we were together as a family. In a strange way, I felt proud that I stood up to Mean Child.

The dirt and dust from the tussle, the bruising from the punches, the freedom to speak my thoughts gave me a sensation I had not known before, the sensation of manly pride. Mother might have to pay for my error, though. Then I wondered: who would have stolen the coyote hanging outside behind our dome, and why would they want it? It made no sense. A thief in the village would most certainly be persecuted and sent to Nothingness if the owner of the belonging wished it. Would One Without wish it? I knew that I had not taken the coyote, though the previous night it was my intention. So who then?

The longer I thought on our dilemma, the more tired I grew from the tea, and I quickly fell into a deep, undisturbed sleep, except for the dreams of tall structures, rolling domes and a leisure life. Mother awakened me well before dusk had fallen, still angry, a look of deep hurt in her brown eyes.

"You need to get up, Moon Child. Let me check your nose," she turned my head this way and that, gently pressing the soft tissue below my eyes. "It looks much better. Another poultice should do it," she replaced it, right as always because I felt much better and could see better, little intrusion of swelling interrupting my view.

"At first night, we have to report to the Wise One. No playing tonight, sorry. That stupid, stupid man has reported his coyote gone, of all things. He is convinced that you stole it. Stupid man!" she spit out, as a bitter piece of fruit.

"But, Mother, I didn't. I wasn't even near it last night. I was at ..." I caught myself, but not before she noted my slip.

"You were where?"

Thinking quickly, I answered, "At my special place. You saw me there. The fight was there."

She looked at me curiously, "Wise One will ask you where you had been and she will know if you are lying, Moon Child."

My head hung, my bare toes wiggled on the dirt floor, "It was my special place." I was doomed to the punishment of the village if I could not come up with something better than that.

"Well, eat your meal, clean up and get dressed. We must hurry. And Moon Child?"

"Yes, Mother?"

"I'm so sorry that I chose poorly for the Joining."

"That's all right, Mother."

Dark settled in before we left the dome and it crept about our ankles during the walk over. Mother tensed, for day workers rarely came out at night, but I felt free, as always. We arrived at the door of Wise One and Mother called, "We are here!" at which point the flap was thrown back, allowing us in. The dome smelled wonderful, of drying herbs, cooking stew, and fresh earth.

"Yes, yes, I understand your claim, Coyote Hunter, but have you proof? You must have proof," Wise One stated. "Ah, yes, come, come Great Builder, Moon Child. You are welcome. Come, sit. We have a problem to solve, apparently, so perhaps Moon Child can shed some light on this little spat?" She patted the earth next to her, urging me to sit there. Coyote Hunter sat on the opposite side. "Tell me Moon Child, what would a boy such as you do with a carcass?"

"Uhm, I have no use for a carcass, Wise One."

"Exactly!" she peered over her other shoulder at Coyote Hunter.

"But the boy was seen last evening during the Joining reaching out for the coyote carcass behind his mother's dome. I have a witness."

"Your son?"

"Yes."

"I see. And how do you answer to that, Moon Child?"

"I just wanted to touch it, feel its fur. I have not touched a dead coyote before." That was the truth.

"Curiosity, you see. That's all, Coyote Hunter."

"But that thing, that boy, became angry at my son for sneaking up on him, very defensive, which proves..."

"Nothing," Wise One finished for him. A messenger burst into the dome before Coyote Hunter could respond, sucking in air after the run across the village.

"Wise One, there is a report of the carcass. It was found in the woods, slashed and torn, insides eaten. Hungry prey, it seems."

"Ah, yes, which would mean the knot must not have been tied properly; which would mean the missing carcass is not the blame of Moon Child, here, but of your own foolishness, Coyote Hunter," her head bowed, punctuating the statement, ending the meeting.

"But I did not tie the knot, Wise One, it was..."

"Yes?" her head bounced upward, a slight smile of pity filling her face.

"Nothing, Wise One," Coyote Hunter glared anger at his son, who jumped from his corner and fled out of the dome in a heated rush to get away from his father, from everyone.

"This hearing is over. I suggest you take some disciplinary measures regarding that boy of yours, Coyote Hunter. Great Builder, given recent events, I suggest *you* take your time thinking through your problem. It is quite possible this Joining was a serious mistake and will not at all benefit the village, in which case you will have six Moons to join another."

I could not believe Wise One would openly make such a suggestion before us all. I glanced at Coyote Hunter, his face burning with rage, humiliation and something much deeper I could not identify, for nobody in the village, nobody in my life had looked such emotion in my presence.

I felt sorry for him, for Wise One had thoroughly shamed him in the presence of Mother. Did he deserve such shame? I could not answer my own doubting question.

Wise One excused all of us, Coyote Hunter storming out of the dome, pushing past me and stopping to glare revenge at Mother. I feared his plans, but I knew Mother's safety secure as long as she remained in the village, for no man in the village had rights to beating neither his wife, nor any wife her husband. As soon as Mother excused me, I ran to the only place I could find answers: Moon Lady.

My feet beat the path toward the other end of the village, the end with our dome. Past our dome I ran, free again, somewhat dizzy with exhilaration, and I suppose, the slight swelling still protruding my nose. Headed for the well-worn path behind our dome, toward my old friend, my lonely friend, the one like me, pale white and glistening with the light of the Moon, I ran without care, forgetting cautions heaped upon me by Moon Lady.

At the edge of the forest, where my old friend lay waiting, I froze in my tracks. Where the delicate Moonflower once stood, small and bright, surrounded by green, only bare ground remained. The laugh brought me back to my senses. The evil, taunting laugh led my eyes up from the ground and into those wicked, mean eyes that most recently tormented me, and down again, from the face to the shoulder, down the arm to the hand ending in short, stubby fingers that held my friend, my once beautiful, brilliant, beckoning friend, already beginning to wilt.

It was then that it happened. It was then, that moment in time that I would undo if I could. It was then that made me wish I had never broken the pact I had made with Mother.

21

As Moon shed its rays down upon the tiny, powerful flower in the hand of evil, and the rays worked their way up, up, up toward the face of the felon, fury built within me, a rage I had never before felt, and had only just seen in the dome of the Wise One.

With every muscle of my being I ran, plunging head first into the stomach of Mean Child who now held my friend, ready to pluck away the first petal.

I felt my head make contact with his hard belly right before we both flew backward onto the compacted ground. I looked up when we first hit, watching as the tiny Moon beams bouncing off the Moonflower worked their way toward his nostrils, just as the light began to enter the orifices of his head, his neck snapped backward from the landing and hit hard upon the ground.

I grabbed the flower from his limp hand, redirecting the tiny rays to my own being, but one single beam remained. One shining thread had already begun the process. I stared down at Mean Child lying on the ground, his eyes beginning to glass over, a fist sized, blood soaked rock pillowing his still head; one tiny beam connected us both to the flower, joining us in life and death.

My eyes glossed over, too, but with tears for my tiny, bright friend, for my thoughtless actions.

Protect the Secrets of the Moon always, Moon Lady's voice repeated in my mind.

Does that mean killing someone to protect it?

That is what will happen to Moon Thief.

Should I heal Mean Child? Could I? Wouldn't the flower do that? Is he dead? What if he is evil and I bring him back? What if he is Moon Thief?

Stop the line!

Would I be bringing him back for my own protection from the village for taking a life? If I did bring him back, would my own protection be a selfish reason?

I felt the evil within me reeling with joy.

I felt the good in me crying, fading, shedding away its skin.

I felt the moonbeams tingling about my head.

I felt the power, a rush of immense power.

I felt the evil rising, the twin years gone, dead, buried within me.

Flash of the past, yet the future, Mean Child lying upon a bed of white sheets.

Flash of the present, I stand over Mean Child drawing Moon's powers, his powers, mine, together as one.

Confusion bounced thoughts around in my mind, stones from a slingshot ricocheting in a canyon.

Ribbons of Moon beams completed their mission into our minds, our bodies, our souls, darkening my vision again, darkening the act, darkening my world.

I stared down at him, lying there, wondering: will he awaken now? Or do I need to bring him back? Should I? Is he the evil one, or am I? Wishful thinking, a blink of his eyes, *blink again, please, just blink, Mean Child*!

I did not want to make this decision. I could not follow my heart.

How easy it is to save the life of one you love, one who would not betray you. How difficult the decision is to make for one like him.

Save him?

Don't save him?

Protect the Moon?

Did I?

Confusion rapped at my heart, my soul, my mind, nothing to follow the questions but confusion, nowhere to turn for answers.

I didn't know what to do, so I started where I

had stopped, on the path to Moon Lady's, my nose aching from the collision, my conscience aching from the action, my heart aching for my friend carried now in my hand. I ran.

22

"Where are you going?" the voice halted me, a stone wall in the forest. Familiar, yet cold, panicked, different, it stopped my running, froze my actions.

My head throbbed. My nose throbbed. I couldn't think. *Who is it? Whose voice?*

I searched the darkness, worriedly; someone had seen the fight. Someone knows I killed Mean Child. They are already after me.

"Where are you going? You must turn back!

Go back!"

Nothing in the darkness, no visage to put with the voice, no face. I saw no face as I turned around searching. They're afraid to show themselves, afraid I will kill them, too.

No light in the deepest forest, only light above, the Moon shining as always, the Moon beating down on the forest trying to break through the thickness of it all. I stared up at the light above the trees, barely filtering through them, the light that slowly began to disappear, the light that faded before my eyes.

"Go back, before it is gone, completely!"

"What is gone?" I yelled at the trees. "Who speaks? Show yourself to me!"

Nothing. I knew the voice. I knew it, but confusion kept me from speaking the name. Evil reared within, blocking my memory, my knowledge, and my choice.

The light withered more and more, slowly, slowly until darkness rose about the treetops, too, the Moon leaving, now half gone. Evil laughed within me.

Confusion, so much confusion filled my body, my mind, my heart. I did not know what was happening. The power reeled in me, but what was I to do? I fell to my knees in the middle of the forest, grabbed my head in my hands, tried to focus my thoughts calling out for help. Huge shining structures whizzed around in my mind.

"Go back! Fight the confusion, the urges of evil! Save the boy! Save the Moon! Go back!"

I twisted my body from the direction of the quartz dome, leaves crunching beneath my knees, dirt grinding into my robe.

I turned from the comfort and answers I sought, the confusion losing to clarity.

I whirled back toward the village, my faltering thoughts gaining ground toward Mean Child, laying in wait for healing to return to the living, my nose throbbing, my knees stinging, the pounding in my head a drum of victory.

A soft, wet tongue touched my cheek, followed by a furry rub from a long snout below my chin. A paw shoved into my arm, sliding downward, the ache of the claws demanding my attention.

A transparent woman in a white robe knelt before me, there in front of me, but not, taking me by the elbows, lifting me gently to my feet, lifting my hand to lead me in the right direction, out of my confusion.

"Go now, before it is too late. Go now!"

Racing time, I returned to the killing place.

23

Mean Child's cold forehead lay beneath my hand; a tear dropped off my chin onto his. I searched the sky for the Moon, barely visible, but still there; I searched the edge of the forest for villagers, nobody, all asleep. I could not believe Coyote Hunter did not search for his son.

I spread my hands over Mean Child's lifeless body, closed my eyes, reached to the quarter Moon above with my heart, my near lifeless friend in my hand, and began the healing, the resurrection, doubtful that I could do it. I had heard stories of a great resurrection, long ago, in another time and place, stories over open fires after wonderful village feasts, the first killing of meat. I had heard stories, but they were not about me resurrecting. They were about the Great One and his own resurrection.

I felt Moon's power contact my fingers, though weak from its shrinking, and I reached for the power with every ounce of my being, drawing it to me, pulling it deeper within, believing with my entire soul that I could perform this very important task. My body shook with the effort.

The light was so dim, the Moon almost fading away, yet as I drew its powers to myself, as I called upon the Moon for the help I so desperately needed, the light grew brighter, the Moon fuller.

I had made the right choice. I closed my weak eyes against the brightness, my swollen nose pulsing as I squeezed my eyelids together. Through my nearly transparent lids, a ball of light grew around Mean One, still lying limp upon the hard earth.

A moan, simple, faint, full of life, affirmed my success. I had brought him back; Moon had brought him back, to what end, I did not know.

The light left me, cold filling my hands, dark filling my closed eyes, rustling of the earth below me filling my ears, overpowering the thump of my beating heart. I had completed the task. He was alive. I opened my eyes, looking down upon Mean Child just awakening, shaking his head as if from a deep sleep, rubbing his scalp where it had made contact with the large rock.

"What happened?" he looked up at me, the lifeless Moonflower in my hand, dying as I felt I would. Something different shone in his eyes, wonderment, not evil, curiosity, a sort of respect.

"That's what I want to know! What have you done to my son? Beating him again, are you?" Coyote Hunter breathed out, storming up from the edge of the village. Had he seen it all? Had I put Moon at further risk?

"What did you do to him? Why are you laying on the ground? Get up! Fight like a man! Learn to be a man!" Fury built in his face as Mean Child remained on the ground before me, clearly confused. Coyote Hunter started toward me, his face reddened by anger, hatred, contempt for the freakishness that was me.

He lurched forward, grabbing at me with his hands. I dodged. I started. This time I sprinted; I did not look back.

24

"You did well," Moon Lady's urgent look quickened my pace to her. "Hurry, hand me the flower!" She instructed.

"It's dead! It's dead!" I screamed between breaths, tears dampening my glowing cheeks. I handed the tiny flower to her. Delicately, she held its stem just below the petals where its lifeless form lay against her fingers, disappearing into her flesh.

"I came upon Mean Child too late. He stole it

from its home. He knew what it meant to me." I shook my head in disbelief. "I almost killed him."

"You did kill him, but you must remember nothing ever truly dies. Watch."

Through my tears, I watched, as the light from the now full Moon above grew brighter. Moon Lady held the tiny wilted flower at the stem just below the petals. Moon rays shot down upon the field of Moonflowers below my feet, upon me, through me, and quickly back out to the down turned petals of the wilted. As my vision cleared, Moon Lady released the tiny stem, which floated in the rays shooting from my body until the flower began to glow again. Soon after, the revitalized flower took its place among the many in the field around the dome, leaving behind, as it descended, one tiny petal floating in the night before me. I reached out and caught it in my palm.

It saddened me, this tiny petal, but I became more melancholy knowing I would not see the flower beyond the village, my old friend, that it would no longer be there to hear my woes, but at the same time, happiness bounded through me that the tiny flower was finally home, as I would probably never be again.

"Could we not have put it back where it was?" I asked, knowing already the answer Moon Lady would give.

"No. It is time. All forever changes once death and rebirth take place. Tell me, your brother, was he changed after you gave him life again?"

I thought on this question, for I did not have much time to discover any changes before running away from Coyote Hunter.

"I had to leave quickly. Coyote Hunter showed up just as I finished bringing him back. I didn't have enough time with him to notice anything, really."

"Even the slightest change, one you may not immediately remember?"

Closing my eyes, I brought back the resurrection decision, the voice in the woods. "The voice in the woods! You were there! How?"

"Another Secret of the Moon, one you will learn tonight, for now that you are banned from the village..."

"Banned?" I squeaked. "But, Mother!"

"Yes. That is why you will learn how I came to you in the forest while remaining here. You will need to be near your mother, but your own safety, safety from the Moon Thief, is in jeopardy now if you return.

"What changes? Any? Think! There must have been some change!" she ordered, returning to the subject of Mean Child, glancing down at the tiny white petal glowing in my hand.

Banned? Is it possible? I asked myself.

"Think!" she ordered more strongly.

Never before had she seemed so desperate, so harsh were her words that it shocked me and for the first time tonight I really looked into her face. She appeared older, ill, and frailer than ever before. I stared concern at her.

"Do not worry about me!" she commanded. "Think about the boy! What changes?"

I turned my face from her, for if I continued to look at her withered appearance, I would not concentrate on what I needed to see. Closing my eyes again, I recalled returning to Mean Child and sealing my eyes against the bright light. When the light dimmed and he moved, my vision fell upon him. My eyes snapped open and met Moon Lady's weary gaze.

"His eyes! There was some change in his eyes! I just noticed it before Coyote Hunter came upon us."

"Good or bad?" her brows drew together expectantly.

"Good. They had lost the evil."

"Good, good. Did anything else happen I need to know about. Before, after, anything? Did Coyote Hunter see anything?"

"No. I feared that he had, but he thought I was fighting with his son again, beating him up, and he attacked me."

I replayed the events from the time I walked up on Mean Child holding my tiny friend in his grubby hand. The beam from the Moonflower! I told her the doubt I had about the Moonflower's death, the beam entering Mean Child, the rest coming to me.

"Oh, that could be bad, very bad," she turned away and paced toward the quartz dome. "Yes, very bad," she repeated, turning back to me.

"H... how so?" I feared the answer, for I knew at the time that my hesitation in gaining the flower back from him might have repercussions on me, or more importantly, Moon.

"I'm not sure yet, but I have an idea. Now he is both, just as you, and that opens the door for Moon Thief. You two are bound, as brothers... twins," she offered the last word slowly, letting it sink in, both in her mind and mine, before continuing.

"Come," with a wave of her hand she led me to the beginning, the place where the tiny scars were burned into my hands, and the place where I learned that I truly was to become great, as Father told me so long ago. The memory brought a sudden realization to mind that quickly turned to fear.

"Father? Where is he? I have not seen him again tonight. He did not run with me to your dome," my brows drew up in a flash of terror. "Coyote Hunter! His carcass! An animal stole it and now, in his rage, his search for me, he has killed another! Tell me I am wrong!"

The look in her eyes, when she turned to me, did not answer my question.

"I cannot tell you that. I do not know. He may be lurking around the village watching over your mother. You will know momentarily."

"You're lying! You do know! I saw something in your eyes."

"You saw my concern for your attachment to your father. Now is the time for separation, not attachment. You must let him go. You have had a year to let him go, and although you have found him again, he is changed. You are destined to this," she spread her arms wide about the field of glowing white, the sparkling dome, the darkness beyond.

"Now that you are separate from the village, you must separate from all. Learn to trust only yourself. Give me the petal."

Tears fell from my eyes as I thought about her words. I lifted my fist with the petal enclosed and began to open my fingers to hers when I remembered again the next to last sentence she spoke. Quickly I closed my fingers around the petal again, pulled my fist back and searched her face.

"As I have said many times, you are a fast learner," a slight smile creased her distressed face, a slight nod, a simple blink of her eyes, told me all I needed to know. I was ready. I was twelve, and I was ready.

"Bring the petal," she moved to the large stones and stood over them. Grasping the seriousness of the previous events, I followed.

"Sit here," she pointed to the flat rock.

I sat.

"Cross your legs, close your eyes, and think about the village, about your mother."

I did as she instructed, blocking out everything except her voice and thoughts of Mother.

"Place the petal on your tongue. That's it. Curl your tongue around the petal and concentrate. Remember everything you see while you are gone."

Gone? I did as she told me.

What happened next I would not have believed two weeks ago could ever happen to me, a defective, lonely, young boy. Many events had taken place in that short time that I would not have believed.

I felt as if I were two people. I saw myself sitting on the flat rock, cross-legged, meditating on the village, on Mother. I saw Moon Lady standing beside me, anxiously awaiting my return with news. She paced before the sitting me like a caged cat awaiting food. I looked down just as my other self, standing, watching them, became more and more solid. Suddenly, Moon Lady whipped around, noticing the other me standing there.

"Why do you stand there?" she desperately shouted. "Go! Go to the village before it wears off!"

"But, can they see me, too?" My knees shook with fear.

"Only one, perhaps two. Stay hidden as though you are there in body." She directed her hand to my body sitting on the ground. "Go, see what is happening."

I turned. I ran. I did not become winded. I did not bruise my feet, though I traveled faster than ever before. I did not even feel the ground beneath my feet, and with good reason. When I looked down at the ground speeding below me, my feet were not touching it! I discovered that I moved my legs, my feet, unnecessarily.

In spirit only I stood on the outskirts of the village just moments later, for much quicker had I arrived at the village than it took my body to get to the dome hours earlier.

26

Understandably, the new me could fly! I had flown through the trees, dodging and swerving, a night bird seeking prey.

I stood, half-hidden by a huge oak tree, watching the people of the village, every dome being searched, my mother, arms held firmly behind her back, protesting the entry of the team who served as Order Keepers in the village, vehemently repeating that her son was not a witch or a killer.

"Look! The boy stands, he walks! He talks!" She pointed and all eyes turned in my direction. I dodged quickly behind the tree. Had they seen me?

"But he is not the boy I raised! Look at him! He is afflicted! Look at him! Your son did this! I came upon them at the edge of the forest and that freak of yours stood over my son waving his hands about him like some magic maker! He stole my son's soul! Look at him!" Coyote Hunter directed the attention of all to Mean Child, who stood in the village in direct line of the tree. I peeked cautiously around the tree. He had been the target of their gaze, not I.

I watched Mean Child, the gathering about him, as if from above, soon realizing that I sat in the branches of the oak, not even remembering when I had climbed it. Mean Child stood by his father, Herb Lady lifting his eyelids, opening his mouth, lifting his arms and letting them fall to his sides again. No response came from the catatonic boy standing beside his father.

"Where is your son? He must die for this act of

thievery! Soul stealing must be a serious enough offense!" He sought out Wise One, who looked hopelessly at Mother standing bound and crying before our dome.

"I'm afraid, Great Builder, your husband is correct. However, I must wait a period of two suns before I make that decision, Coyote Hunter, for your son could be in a state of shock. Plus, I would like to speak personally with Moon Child. I must have his side of the story."

"He is not here!" An Order Keeper commanded upon exiting our dome.

"Where is he?" Wise One asked of Mother.

"He goes out at night. He is not supposed to go beyond the place where Coyote Hunter found him and the boy earlier, just there. He must be afraid! He broke our pact!"

"Your pact?" Wise One looked confused.

"To not go beyond the edge of the village, beyond the flower that grew there." Mother's tears filled with betrayal, punctuating her words. I wanted to turn myself in to save her this misery. I found I had moved to the ground again, tears filling my own eyes.

"He broke the pact."

She sobbed, falling to her knees, supported only by the two Order Keepers who held her arms.

27

"By order of law, Great Builder must be detained until the boy returns so she cannot alert him!" Coyote Hunter smugly reminded Wise One.

"I know the law, Coyote Hunter. Who is the Wise One here? He is correct, however. Take her to the holding dome immediately, bar the door, and do not leave your post at the entrance, under any circumstances. I do apologize, Great Builder. It is the law."

"Why do you apologize to her? You are the lawmaker and her evil son has broken the law!"

I started to move to Mother, wanted to comfort her, wipe her tears away. I took a step. A face turned in my direction, a smug face filled with revenge and hate. The sneer, the eyes, the nod, told me he had spotted the new me and that this was all a game to him.

The knife he drew from his belt at his waist, however, was no game. It glinted in the Moon's light. He took the point of the knife between rough finger and thumb, looking over the top of Mean Child's head.

He would not even give me an opportunity to explain; he would just kill me without a chance.

If that is what he wanted, the he must be the Moon Thief!

I looked down at my body, trying to determine if an injury could be incurred in this state, and there at my feet was Father. I had not felt him there. I had no feeling. He could not feel me either. If he could, he would know that I stood next to him, for his head leaned into the calf of my right leg, almost halfway through it. There he was, guarding over Mother, lurking, watching, and waiting for an opportunity to save her, but the knife! When I looked up, the knife floated toward him, between Coyote Hunter and Father.

"Run!" I shouted at Father, "Don't be foolish! Run!" I did not know if he would hear me, but I had heard Moon Lady in the forest earlier, so I had to try.

Father's ears perked up, and quickly he ducked away from the knife, which now lay behind me on the ground just past the place where he had stood.

I looked up at Coyote Hunter smugly, but not for long, because Mean Child stared intently at me, though his body stood dumbfounded. He had turned and now glared!

Coyote Hunter pointed.

Mother's eyes widened with wonder.

"There he is, the boy!" Coyote Hunter yelled. It was not almost being caught that frightened me so, though. It was the look that Mean Child shared with me now. As if looking into a mirror, I stared back, the same look of fear. We were one. I flew away before Coyote Hunter and Mother, who had broken free of her holders, reached the spot where I had stood. I disappeared.

My body jerked into motion. All at once, I uncrossed my legs, my head snapped up and I stood upon the flat rock facing Moon Lady. The petal I had held in the curvature of my tongue floated from my slightly opened mouth and returned to the flower from which it had fallen. I stammered, fearful that if I did not tell her everything at once, villagers would surround the dome, the Moonflowers, Moon Lady and I. Angry, vengeful Order Keepers led by Coyote Hunter, tearing apart everything in their path to find me.

"They... saw... me... Mean... Child's... eyes... Coyote... Hunter... knife... imprisoning... Mother... coming! They are coming!" I blurted in one breath.

My eyes searched the forest around the dome, but nothing lurked in the darkness.

"Stop!" Moon Lady placed her fragile hands upon my shoulders, stopping the frantic spinning

I threw myself into trying to get away, trying to locate the hunters.

"They cannot beat you here. Nobody is here. It is, however, as I feared. The boy is one with you. While you projected to the village, he projected here. He wandered the forest around the dome, taking in all that he could, remembering. I watched him, but he could not see me. He could, however see you, because you are one.

"Do not worry about your mother. She will overcome the imprisonment. I know Wise One too well. Worry only about yourself. Right now, you need rest. That type of power from Moon is very exhausting. Let us enter the dome. I have a pallet made up for you. Sleep now." Her hand on my back comforted me enough to follow her to the dome, but thoughts of invasion quickly surfaced again.

"But they will find us! They want to kill me!"

"Only the boy can see you. Moon cast a protective enclosure around the area upon your leaving. The boy will feel as exhausted as you do. It is likely he will not speak until tomorrow. Rest now."

28

I lay down upon the pallet she indicated, and though moments before I had been excited, wide awake and ready to run, I fell immediately asleep.

Past midnight to early next evening, I slept. And I dreamed. And my dream filled my thoughts with greed, with sloth, with gluttony. I did not notice the changes, but Moon Lady did. She watched me as a hawk watches its prey before swooping down, catching the prey in its talons and pulling it apart limb for limb in ravage hunger. She watched every move, listened for every noise, and mentally took note of every habit I developed. I did not care if she watched me, though. When I awoke, I knew what I wanted and what I had to do.

My dream awakened me a different person than earlier when I fell out upon the bedding before dawn.

The buildings! Oh the glorious buildings! They touched the sky with their magnificent rooftops! Their beauty as they glinted and shimmered in the afternoon sun blinded me!

I had visited Mother again, the large dirt-free dome gleaming, the wonderful aroma of the flat cakes settling on my joyous senses, tempting me so that I had to try one. I had visited several times now; I was comfortable here.

I ate at least six of those wonderful cakes that she called cookies. Yes, chocolate chip cookies, peanut butter cookies, wonderful, heavenly cookies, I ate them all!

While I ate, Mother touched a small flat object

and this huge box shaped thing on the wall began to show pictures. Unlike the pictures on the wall, these pictures talked and moved. There are people in the box! I exclaimed, pointing and Mother laughed. I watched the people live their lives in the box. Once, I laughed at some antic or other and turned to see if Mother watched, too. She stood smiling down at me, eating her cookies, drinking a delicious white liquid, and laughing. She and Father stood behind me watching, happy that I had adjusted so well. Father had his arm around her, just as he used to before...

My body subconsciously rolled over, trying to shake out the unpleasant thought of what had really happened to Father, trying to catch hold of the dream again. I remained asleep, but I could feel Moon Lady watching, listening, and hovering over me.

Father asked if I wanted to go for a ride on his motorcycle. I went. I had never ridden anything in my life, until now. I had always walked or ran everywhere. I smiled from ear to ear sitting behind Father, my hands grasping his jacket at the waist.

I was straddling something, a seat of some kind. The black path beneath us sped past. I laughed as I watched white lines blur to my left.

The wind blew my white hair back away from my face! I felt free! Free of all the burdens that had become my life as a Moon Child. The night was dark, but the streetlights, as Father called them, lit our village well. He explained to me again, how we no longer lived in a village, that we lived in a city, a very big city. I repeated his magnificent word, city... city... city, laughing and laughing as we sped through the streets of our new home.

We stopped at a place called a diner where food is cooked. We ate something called hamburgers, French fries and shakes. They were almost as delicious as Mother's cookies, and the hamburger! Full of meat!

Father told me again, how happy he was that I had built this city, because it had made me so happy, and that our lives were so much easier, so much more convenient. I was a changed child, he said. Look at that smile, he said. I told you that

you would be great someday and do great things;
he nodded.

I was so stuffed when we left for home that I
laid my head on his back and almost fell asleep
before we arrived at our new building.

We entered the apartment, as Father called it,
and I went to the window to look out over the city,
my city, the city I had built. Pride filled my heart
until I realized, looking out over this wonderful
place, that if not for the lights provided by this
city, there would be no light at all. I turned to ask
my parents about this discovery, but they were no
longer in the room. Instead, Moon Lady stood
there on shaking knees, watching her world end,
her life end, her head motioning disappointment,
tears inundating the creases in her face.

Suddenly, the lights of the city went out! I
called for Father, for Mother, but neither
answered. The apartment stood in darkness,
silence; the city stood in darkness. Blinded by
nothingness, I stood still, afraid to move any
which way. I turned back toward the window
searching for some way to light my path, but even

life outside the window stood onyx, cold, hopeless. No Moon shone through to give me vision. Moon, always my friend, had gone, leaving me to my laziness, my progress, my destruction. The sky lay dark without horizon.

Melancholy and desire ripped through me when I awoke that evening. I wanted so much of what I had experienced in my dream; in spite of the blindness those luxuries left, curiosity filled me. I suppose that is why I did what I did in the end.

I stepped outside the dome in the new twilight. Shadows filled the forest around the Moonflowers, creeping, stirring, and gliding about the trees. I remembered the village, the Order Keepers, Mother, and nervously began looking for a place to hide as people entered my view.

"They cannot see us. The shield, remember? The boy can sense you, though. Look!" her voice of sadness filled my ears as a crooked finger from over my shoulder guided my attention to where Mean Child stood.

There he peered directly across the Moonflowers from me, looking right at me, as though he could see me through the shield. Suddenly, I thought about these villagers, my village, and wondered about their reaction to a huge city, a city I built, right here, right now, buildings popping up around them. I saw them in my mind's eye, scattering through the trees, running from the buildings that touched the sky, running from the roadways flowing around them, between them, over them, running from the wonderful smells from the diners. Would they be scared or would they want it too?

I watched them search for me now, my eyes resting on Mean Child. He had shared my thoughts through the shield, for his eyes held wonder, his face a smile, and he nodded. He had dreamed of progress, dreamed my dream, or I his, and we were in agreement.

Was it me? Was it him? Did he give me these dreams all along, or was I giving them to him?

I had made up my mind, days ago, that he was the Moon Thief, but now I was certain. He

was waiting for me to choose his side. I could not
have been more wrong as I glanced around at the
rest of the villagers, my eyes resting on another,
one whom I feared not, Mother. The villagers
finally left the forest, the Order Keepers the last
to go, Mother in tow, yet they went home
unsuccessful in their mission.

"Here, this is for you. You can wash, and then
put it on. Your clothes are worn and ripped, not
befitting a Child of the Moon. Go to the creek on
the other side of the dome, beyond the
Moonflowers, and bathe. If any lingers they will
not see you there. Take care not to ripple the
water too much."

A coolness filled Moon Lady's voice that had
never been there before. Did she know of my
dream? Had the change in me shown?

I took the shimmering white robe from her
gently. Its beauty flooded my eyes. I could not
believe it was for me.

Before she walked away from me, I had to
know, "Are you angry with me about what
happened? Have I done something very bad?"

She turned slowly toward me, the sadness still in her eyes, "You've done as you were meant to do. You are as you are supposed to be. Everything is as it must be. I do not care for surprises or unexpected outcomes, but I should be used to them. Moon had its way of teaching me," a thin smile crossed her lips as she glanced up. "People have their ways, too."

She gave me a hard, suspicious look, and then left me to find my way.

How strange an answer? She was not angry with me, but I had surprised her? Is that what she meant? I pondered on her words while I walked to the creek. *Why had she looked at me so?*

29

The cool water in the creek calmed my nerves, my doubts, for a short time, but once I slipped the shimmering white robe over my head and Moon's rays danced upon its surface, a flash here, tiny prisms there, minuscule jewels signaling the Moon, the doubts returned. I spread my hands, palms up, the white robe flowing around me. The tiny scars in my palms filled with light, pulsing, warming, and building for a final battle.

Did I deserve such an honor? Was I truly a Moon Child? How could I fight the urges left behind by the miraculous dreams haunting me?

On the walk back to the quartz dome, cookies entered my mind. I tried to recall how they tasted in my dream. Moreover, views of my family together again in the huge dome, together and happy, filled my thoughts. That was the key, wasn't it?

I looked up at Moon as I stood atop the beautiful white flowers sent to us for our resurrection and preservation, my arms spread pleadingly. "That is the key, isn't it?"

I solemnly peered up, waiting for an answer I did not expect to come, an answer I already knew.

My family was the key to the dream, the urges and desires that filled me. I wanted what I had had in my youth, but with greater happiness, and there had been so much happiness in my dream, until...

Did Moon just shrink?

Surely, it had been my imagination while I

tried to block the memory of the darkness that followed the joy in my dreams.

Certainly, Moon's light did not falter for even the smallest of moments.

Fear entered my heart again, the end of the dream filling my mind, chasing away the urges and desires the big city left in me.

Shoulders slumped, I returned to the dome, my dome of the future, no Mother, no Father, no happiness, no cookies. Moon Lady set out a feast, but I could not muster the hunger to eat.

"You must eat. You need to keep up your strength. The end is coming closer, the great battle between Dark and Light, and you will need your own strength of youth as well as that of the Moon." She pushed my plate back toward me forcefully.

Something was wrong. She acted so strangely. Perhaps I should speak to her about my dream, warn her of my urges. Brows drawn together, I looked up, opened my mouth to speak, but my words were stopped by a motion caught in the corner of my eye.

Out the door of the dome, I glimpsed a coyote running around the edge of the Moonflowers.

"Father!" I jumped from my seat at the table and ran out the door to greet him, but he did not come to greet me. He ran one direction around the flowers, then turned and ran the other direction.

"Come back and eat. He cannot enter through the shield," Moon Lady instructed from the dome.

"Can't you let him in?" I begged.

"No. I am not the one who is protecting this dome. There is no power greater than Moon's; I am only a servant to that power, a conduit of it. I channel it when it is needed, as will you."

My shoulders dropped; my head lowered; my feet dragged me back to the table. The dream would never be mine, for Moon had chosen my path and it was to be one of sheer and utter loneliness, no family, no buildings, no life. I felt much too young for the choices Moon was asking me to make now.

I picked at my food as I watched Father run circles around the shield, just as I had ate cookies and watched television in my dream.

"Why has Moon taken everything from me?"

Moon Lady's head jerked up, anger filling her quickly reddening face, "Never again say that! Moon is the provider of all the good in your life! Moon does not take away! People take away! Moon has not done this to you! I have!" She rose and stormed out of the dome.

That is where her anger came from. She was angry with herself, angry because she rushed in her task to act as Moon wanted.

Feeling slightly better, yet sorry for her, I picked at my food until she returned.

"I'm sorry for my outburst, Moon Child. My decision has tormented me all these years, and now the fruition of my deeds will come to be. I know not what will happen, and I don't like not knowing. Moon knows not what will happen. Only you, child, can know what you will do, and I see in your face, in your sleep, in your actions, that you do not even know what you will do, and I am scared. I am scared, because you must be separated from all you love to make your decision. I am scared because you must fight this fight of good and evil alone. I am scared because within you both good and evil reside; your heart is the only one that can win over to one side, and you know not where your heart will go.

"You must be alone and away from all influence to make this decision, though. It must be yours to live with forever, as mine has been. I see in your eyes the desire for progress, for change, for ease of ways, though to me nothing could be easier than the way life is now, and has been for hundreds of years. I am scared, but you must earn the right to become the next Protector of the Moon, and you must do it alone. You are ready; Moon knows you are ready."

I did not feel ready. After her speech, I was more confused than ever before. "If Moon locks me away like this, then how am I to catch the Moon Thief?"

"You have the means. You have the powers of Moon. When the time comes, when the shield lifts, Moon Thief will be locked away in the onyx dome, or not."

I pushed away my plate and went to sit among the flowers; sadly, I watched Father run in circles, trying hard to find me, to reach me. I needed him.

I needed Mother. They had always helped me make my decisions. I could not reach out to them now. I watched; he ran.

For several nights, locked up within the shield

of the Moon, only Moon Lady and myself, we wandered without much speaking. For several nights, I meditated, searching for the truth, the future, a glimpse of the choice I would make. For several days, I dreamed, the dreams getting stronger, the urges growing, the events more plentiful and powerful. Was this how I was to spend time with my family again, only in my dreams? Was this the only way for me not to be alone?

I was not alone, though. Moon Lady remained with me. She hovered in my sleep. She showed her concern in my meditations. Her eyes wished she had not made the mistake she had made, that my life, her life, would not be so difficult. She did not speak, a ghost filling my nights, like Moon above, a ghost of the life I used to live before I had killed Mean Child and brought him back to life.

He came every evening, Mean Child, staying almost until dawn, searching for a way around the shield, a way to get to me. He was not angry. He no longer looked mean. He was changing physically, too. Every day, he more resembled me, my twin in truth. Something strange was happening, and I did not understand it.

31

One evening, after I had awakened, I dared to move to the inside edge of the shield. I looked directly into his dark eyes, but no sign of the old Mean Child remained. He no longer bullied other children, he guided them, and I saw that through his thoughts.

He peered directly through the shield, as if seeing me. He peered into my eyes, sensing my indecision; concern for me creased his brow, for with my indecision came his indecision.

We were one.

We felt together the pains, the agonies, and the

choices. I wondered, truly, what choice he would make, so I devised a test.

I closed my eyes, envisioning the objects of my dreams, first the cookies, the flavor of them, the warm sweetness as they melted in my mouth. So strong were the sensations, that when I opened my eyes his tongue flipped around his lips seeking crumbs.

My confusion grew.

Moon Lady stood behind me. I did not know she was there, or for how long she watched us, until she spoke, "Did you expect something else from him? He is you; you are he. He feels what you feel, sees what you see, your twin, yourself."

She turned and walked away, leaving me more bewildered than before I had ventured into this test. It was the next evening when I awoke that my decision began to take shape, my mistake taking form.

32

I had not felt Moon Lady hovering in my dreams, and this dream seemed the happiest, the most joyful of all others. Yet, she had not been there watching me.

I awoke in haste, missing the security I had felt previously while I dreamed, the grounding she had given me while joy flooded my days of sleep.

Where could she be? Where had she gone?

Had she, too, given up on me, leaving me to

my own tortured demise?

I ran from the dome in search of her, not going far before I spotted her upon the flat rock where it all began, where first she sliced my palms. The star shaped scars tingled with the memory.

There she sat, the same position I had sat in to travel outside my body. Perhaps she did the same now. Perhaps she needed the comfort of knowing what happened around us. Villagers had given up the search for me, the only visitor being Mean Child, who knew exactly where I was at all times.

I approached her motionless, pale body, sitting cross-legged on the flat rock, her head bowed as in sleep, her fingers intertwined in her lap. Long gray hair hung loose, falling about the sides of her face, her shoulders, and her knees. Peace filled her, settled about her, an opaque egg of light protecting her.

I sat upon the Moonflowers opposite her, watching, waiting for a sign of her return, but there was none.

I sat, I watched, and I began to fear. Moon sat

high in the sky, yet I had not moved, nor had she. I reached out to her. Perhaps touching her would let her know I was here and she would return, but such coldness burned my fingers, that I withdrew my hand before it had broken through the light.

Hours passed as Moon grew brighter in the night sky, filling her bubble with light. I watched the protective light grow brighter and brighter, no motion from within to burst it.

Is this what happened to me when I traveled?

The brightness grew and grew, until I had to shield my eyes from the glare, keeping Moon Lady in my blurred vision. Without warning, without sign from Moon, a flash so strong, an explosion of sorts, blew me backwards onto the Moonflowers.

When I regained my position, pushing myself back up, when I opened my burning eyes, she was gone. She had not been traveling.

She had gone to the flat rock to die, the last lesson I was to learn from her regarding my position in life.

Now I was completely alone, alone to do battle with one I could not find, one I could not identify. Words filled my ears, faint, yet powerful words. Words I recognized.

Beware the joy!

33

Tears spilled upon the flat rock, her final resting place, as I cried. My hands searched, stroked, crept along the flat rock hoping to find some remnant that would make it untrue, but all my trembling fingers found were the wet drops falling, falling, falling.

Grief flooded me.

I could not eat, though every evening, as though she were still with me, the table filled with food. I could not sleep, though with every dawn weariness overtook my body. I could not trust in myself, though I was alone and apparently ready to fill my new position and capture the Moon Thief. Now a man, tears dampened the bedding where my head lay, just as they had when I was a child listening to the children play outside my window in Mother's dome.

Mother.

I wondered where she was, what was happening to her, if she were imprisoned still? I thought of the mother in my dreams, so happy, so alive, so filled with love for her family.

Father.

I wondered if he circled the village, watching over her, ears perked, tongue hanging, tail drooping, stalking, listening. He had not been here for many nights. I thought of him, adventurous, boyish in the new world I dreamed, happy as Mother and filled with as much love.

Even Mean Child had not returned. Mean Child who had stood outside the shield for three days and nights, though I would not come to him. He had cried my tears, he had felt my pain, and for three days and nights, he had grieved with me, never leaving me, but I stayed away from him. For I knew when the time came, I would have to imprison him in the onyx dome, and getting closer to him, though how we could be any closer I did not know, would make that time all the more difficult. Yet, still he had remained until now, the time of battle growing closer, the tension within the shield growing thicker, Moon's brightness at its best, its most powerful.

The time was here and all I remembered were the last words Moon Lady spoke as she left me, *'Beware the joy!'*

What was I to do? For the joy is exactly what I wanted from my dream, joy unlike that I had ever known. Alone and fighting the uncertainty of what had happened to everyone I loved, what would happen to everyone I loved, I made the decision to take another trip to the village, the beginning of my end.

I folded my legs and sat upon the warm flat

rock where Moon Lady had left this world, and me, days before. I watched my hand reach for the tiny, shimmering petal of the Moonflower closest to me.

Power surged through my fingers, up my arm, into my heart as I lifted the petal to my rolled tongue. I lowered my head, envisioning the village.

I was there.

Walking cautiously about the edge of the village, beginning at the back of Mother's dome, I listened. Loud voices reached my ears, but not from near our dome. They came from the other side of the village, the Wise One's dome.

Though almost transparent, I sneaked along the outskirts of the village, around the circular clearing, hiding behind the trees.

When I reached the dome, the angry voice of Coyote Hunter filled my ears.

"She must be imprisoned! Someone has to pay. Look at him! It has happened again this very night. He is not with us. His soul is gone! Look! Are you blind, woman?"

"How *dare* you speak to me in that tone!" Wise One's voice trembled with rage and power. "We have questioned him when he was alert and here. He does not provide us with any information that lends to your argument! You have no proof!"

"Looking at him should be proof enough! Someone has to pay and since her freakish son is gone, then it must be her!" Through the tiny window, I saw him point viciously at Mother, who stood with head bowed, defeated and bound.

"You are correct in that argument. There is something wrong. If only he could speak, tell us the truth so that I knew the right decision, Great Builder. For now, I suppose you will have to remain imprisoned."

A hearing with Mother bound and saddened at the turn her life had taken. I could not bear it! I looked for Mean Child, his body again limp, sitting there on the dirt floor, legs crossed, head bowed, just as I had left my own body on the flat rock.

How could I make him speak, get Mother free of the charges that Coyote Hunter made? I needed to find him, talk to him, make him go back. There was no time. How could I fix this?

I had to think of something. If only I could inhabit Mean Child long enough to speak for him, to make it right, for it was my fault after all, all of it was my fault.

Suddenly, I slipped into darkness, my eyes snapped open, and Mother stood in my vision, head bowed. Her eyes met mine hopefully and filled with joy.

"She is innocent. Her son is innocent. I picked a flower outside the village, a beautiful white flower and the poison within it brought this punishment to me," I heard myself, in the voice of Mean Child, report.

"You lie!" A fist caught me in my right temple, Mean Child's right temple, causing excruciating pain, and then no pain, only darkness, again.

35

The next morning, I slept. Grief, loneliness and my trip to the village had exhausted me. In my first hour of slumber, no dreams filled me, only darkness, peace, and weariness so great no visions could penetrate it, as well as the steady drumming in my head.

Soon, however, the darkness left and the dreams began again. For a time I would not be alone. *I had Mother and Father, and this time I had a friend. A friend stayed over in our new home, and we played games, laughing and wrestling with each other.*

Games, unlike any of the village games, filled our time together.

We held some type of controls in our hands, controls hooked up to a box that was connected into a television. We played against each other. Then we took a break and ate Mother's wonderful cookies, licking away the crumbs from our smiling faces, from our fingers, our clothes.

We had so much fun together. We pulled pranks on Father while he napped and we laughed with Mother after he awakened, roaring and chasing us around the apartment.

It was not until my own joyful laughter brought me to consciousness that I realized the friend was none other than Mean Child, who had become my twin, my brother.

I jerked myself up from my bedding, suddenly filled with ravage hunger, the joy of the dream still upon me, within me, cracking my face with a smile.

I had been so tired; I did not even remember the trip back to the quartz dome, or falling into my bedding. It must have been the blow to my head, Mean Child's head that caused this lack of memory.

36

Newly famished, I ate ravenously from the feast at the table, filling the emptiness within, but I realized that the flavor I truly sought could not be found among the wonderful food upon the table. I ached for a cookie, but I still filled my hunger. As I tipped a cup to my lips, my eyes moved up toward the door, and there, watching me, just outside the dome, stood Mean Child. He looked healthy, well, no marks upon his temple. He was different.

The cup slipped from my hand, spilling the contents of the sweet fruit juice upon the food, bouncing off the table, and coming to rest upon the floor at my feet as I stood.

How had he penetrated the shield?

How had he gotten through?

Did I bring him here in my dream?

Was it my trip to the village?

So visible was the fear in my eyes that it reflected in his, and he jumped back, as did I. Backing slowly away from each other, he toward the edge of the Moonflowers and I into the wall behind me, we did not let our gaze upon each other falter. Then I realized that he stood over the Moonflowers as I had, and he did not trample them.

What was happening?

How was it that he could walk upon them as I did? It was not possible, unless he too was ... It couldn't be!

I looked into his eyes, his face slightly darker than mine, his dirty blonde hair, the once complete opposite of myself, yet me beneath the surface.

I moved slowly toward him, and he back toward me, though much slower. He allowed me to exit the arch of the quartz dome, step out onto the Moonflowers, now glowing with Moon's light, and close the short distance between us, the dancing rays from the Moonflowers lighting our surprised faces, giving them an eerie, magical glow that increased our fear.

I looked about us, the night flooding us.

When had it gotten so dark? Had I slept that long, dreamed that long?

Of course, I must have. I had not slept for three days. Certainly, I was so tired that a whole day, if not two, must have passed while I was sleeping. Surely, the weak state of my malnourished body completely wiped me out.

Inches apart, we stared at each other, into each other's eyes, into each other's soul, the sadness of what must come to be filling our hearts. He was completely calm now, as calm as I. Through our eyes, we communicated our feelings for each other, feelings that had developed during the time of grief and probably well before that, beginning when I had first killed him and then saved him.

We knew, each of us knew, that his would be the last time we would be together, be one person, yet two. The greater plan had already been set in motion, and one of us would not be here after this night. We looked up at the Moon together, basking in the light surrounding us, the comfort it brought us, the power.

Remembering the dream of the day, I smiled at him. He returned my smile, his teeth white against his complexion; mine slightly yellowed in comparison to my bright skin. He did not cringe at my smile, at my skin, as he did when we first met.

He did not shout, "Freak!" at me. I knew he had changed, become my brother, my friend, but it was not meant to be.

Last night we had changed our positions, somehow switched places, though. He had been here, living my life, as I lived his for only the short moments that I was gone.

Perhaps the trip had made him more understanding of me, I of him. We had already become one, and now the oneness felt so much deeper. I was saddened that it could not remain so.

We moved closer to each other, the joy within exuding a glow only enhanced by Moon. The barrier between his world, a world we once shared, and my world, now lifted.

Laughter filled our ears, each other's laughter, as we remembered the games, the pranks, and the fun of the dream filled day. Before we knew it, our arms encircled each other in a brotherly hug, each laughing in the other's ear. We were together.

He had mysteriously become my twin, the twin taken from me before birth, the brother lost to me upon Moon's wishes.

I invited him in without words. We finished off the food together, no conversation filling the air about us, for we thought the same.

White apples, meat, milk and honey glided

over our tongues, through our teeth, beyond our smiles. Delicious food left us longing for more.

37

Only occasional laughter split the sound barrier from time to time as we remembered and devised and planned.

It was not until after the meal, after the fun, after the loneliness within me had died, that I made the decision. He knew, understood, and agreed. One of us would go; one of us would stay. Did it have to be that way? We moved out and stood in the open brightness of the Moon, upon the Moonflowers glowing with apparent reverence.

Our hands joined, smiles splitting our faces from ear to ear. Was it an illusion I saw behind my brother? He turned to look.

There stood Mother, a smile filling her face, too. Beside her, sitting on his haunches, her hand resting upon his head, sat Father.

Next to him, several feet away, stood Coyote Hunter, a scowl upon his face, tormented by the bond formed between his son and me.

I glimpsed Father again, sitting there, growling, and keeping Coyote Hunter at bay whenever he attempted to move toward us.

Would Father change back when I fulfilled my purpose? Perhaps I should change him now. Mean Child nodded at me.

I lifted my hands to the Moon.

My palms' scars burned with light.

Joy flooded my heart.

The ball of light formed, and Father moved into it. The transformation complete, Mother tossed him a robe and they fell into each other's arms.

Coyote Hunter stood slack jawed. Nevertheless, he took this opportunity to advance toward Brother and me, but Father soon turned, ran after him, and tackled him.

They fought.

Coyote Hunter fell backward on a boulder, the back of his skull red and matted, as once was his son's. In a fluid motion, Father knelt to check him, his blood from the head wound staining the grass just beyond the Moonflowers.

The first words I spoke to my brother since he had penetrated the shield were, "Shall I heal him?"

His first and last word spoken to me was, "No."

We wanted the same thing. We wanted the same life. We wanted the parents that belonged to us, and the life we could have together.

Mother wanted it.

Father wanted it.

The desire grew within me and as it did, so did Mean Child's smile, reflecting my own.

Neither of us had to die, imprisoned forever.

38

There was a way, there was power, and that power could change our world, change the decisions, and change our family.

The only vision in my mind was that of those I loved most, of the city I was to build for them, for our happiness together, of the greatness my father promised me as a young child.

Never to be alone again, that was my dream, the dream I had had since I began to dream. I realized that now. Loneliness had not been a part of any of my dreams.

Giving Mother and Father all they had wanted, giving them back their son who had been so wrongfully stolen from them before his birth, giving them back both sons who had been taken from them for the purpose of Moon and its protection against progress, was all that I thought about now, that, and cookies.

Moon Thief, and the darkness he would bring, now a distant memory pushed down by the idea of a beautiful, new, shining city, a wonderful, happy family life unlike that either of us brothers had known. We would be complete again, Father, Mother, Brother and I, together as one family, as we should be. In my mind's eye, the shining city formed before us, around us, within us.

I raised my hands to the Moon.

My scars burned with light.

The brightness blinded me.

The circle of light grew around me, around us. Tall buildings began to form, pushing up out of the earth. Streets began to roll through the trees, winding around them, beneath their night-darkened shadows. In my mind, the beautiful new shining city grew all light and amazing, and from my mind, the city began to take shape about me. Buildings, glorious buildings, reached for the moon.

The Moon?

My feet touched a cold surface!

Progress already begun, the cold floors must be smashing the delicate Moonflowers beneath them, crumbling them to dust!

I looked down at my feet, where no flowers grew, only darkness, blacker than that of night.

When my eyes moved up, a strong wall of darkness began to grow around the start of my city, an onyx wall.

Mother screamed!

Father cried out, "Stop!"

A single faint word rang through my ears, into my conscience, but it was too late!

Mean Child stood fixed upon the same street as I, right where it ended, next to Mother and Father, hands raised to the Moon, like mine, a similar look filling his paling face. The three watched from the other side of the growing wall.

How had my brother gotten there? How had Mother and Father gotten there? When had Mean Child moved to stand next to them? When had the change taken place?

His hands rose further up to the Moon, tiny scars on his palms glowing, light building around him, increasing, blinding light. He had stolen my powers, Moon's powers!

No!

No!

How had he tricked me?

I raised my hands higher, reaching as never before to the powers of Moon, squeezing my eyes against the brightness produced from the draw of power between us, the Moon glowing like never before!

He could not get away with this! I could not let him steal the powers from me!

The onyx wall grew, and try as I might I could not stop it.

I peered at my open palms.

No light flooded them.

No pink scars lined them.

Below my feet, no Moonflowers glowed, all darkness.

My friend, my family, my life, gone, they were all gone. Soon my dream would be gone, too, lost to me forever!

The last I saw them, my family, before my eyes pleaded with Moon until the end, I saw Mother and Father embracing my brother, Moon Child, while he completed his task, their laughter and joy evident. They were happy to be together again; soon they would turn toward the quartz dome.

My brother, the new occupant of the gleaming white structure, his hair glowing whiter, his skin glistening lighter, the pure robe now shining about his body, basked in the light reflecting up from the Moonflowers below my family.

My brother shone like no other in the village!

In spite of myself, and my destiny, I was proud.

The three entered the dome together, Moon Child's new home, where he would live out the rest of his days, keeping Moon's secrets, keeping the new ways, and detaining progress for another generation. I watched them through blurred eyes until the onyx wall grew so tall that the last little circular hole in the roof filled with Moon, wavering in my tears; Moon, whom I had betrayed for joy. I watched as my old friend grew smaller with the shrinking of the hole, entombing me within.

Only one dream I would know now, in the bright,

beautiful city I had begun to create, the city of the foundation that now surrounded me, the city of my dreams, my city enclosed in darkness.

The reality of this one dream brought a truth from my trembling, repentant lips.

"Darkness, *I* am Moon Thief!"

Note from the Author

I hope you enjoyed Moon Thief. I know it was complicated at times, especially the naming of Moon Child and Mean Child. I wanted to emphasize the good and evil in each of us, how fine that line is, and therefore kept their names closely linked.

I could really use your help now that you've read *Moon Thief.* If you would be so kind as to post a review of this book at the following sites, I would be forever in your debt. It means the world to me for my readers to share their thoughts about my work with others.

Thank you.

https://www.amazon.com/dp/1712581201/
r#customerReviews
https://www.facebook.com/AuthorPGShriver/
reviews
https://www.barnesandnoble.com
http://www.goodreads.com

A Gift for You

Hey, hey! It's me again! I told you at the beginning that I like to give away items to my readers. On the next page you'll find the first chapter of my Teen Superhero Fantasy, <u>Paradise Rising</u>. It's the first book in thegiftedonestrilogy.com . You can find all you need to know about those books at that link. Enjoy!

S creams... were they part of the dream? A tiny wet caress on her bare shin, her elbow, and then her chin, attempted to wake her.

Trying to shake off both the dream and the licks, she rolled away hoping to stay asleep, hoping to see him this time, the faceless man. Her need to see his face was strong, though she wasn't sure why. She felt, in her semi-awakened state, that he was connected to her life, to the tragedies that had occurred, the loneliness, but she had no factual assurance, only intuition, and the dream.

More screams pierced the sleep induced silence, stirring her—distant, torturous screaming that had never before presented itself in the dream.

She rolled away from more intermittent moist tickles, a cool dampness running over her arm, and in her sudden urge to remain asleep, she fell off the hard metal park bench onto the dew soaked grass beneath it.

No staying asleep now. She raised up on her elbows, wiping wet grass from her face while frowning at the little mutt, her companion in hiding for the past few days. He shook the dew drops from his multicolored coat, spraying her with wet dog water.

Not fully awake, she stood—wiped fruitlessly at

dampened skin—and rubbed at the chill on her bare arms.

"Thanks, buddy!" She scoffed at the dog.

Glancing beyond the early dawn, darkness still surrounding the park, street lights sparkling the dense fog, circular areas of grass glistening with moisture, she stretched her cold, stiff muscles. The chill of the morning seeped under her skin, gripped her muscles and caused tiny tremors throughout her body.

Damp to her soul, she looked down at the pitiful dog. Screams echoed through the dark background. Her vision tunneled, blackening around the edges. "Not again," she whispered.

The screams, the moans of pain, the weak cry for help, called to her, chose her course, started her in motion, running, building speed, though she didn't realize it; she was already gone, drawn within herself into the darkness.

It was happening more and more frequently, the screaming, the black outs, the memory loss. Physically, she ran; mentally, she stood silent, in that all too familiar place of shadows.

Led without control to an unknown destination, as always, she followed.

Returning to the early morning light of a world her body never left and to the sounds of the city around her, she blinked repeatedly, focusing her eyes to the dim alleyway where she stood. Crammed and filthy, homeless people slept about her in cardboard boxes, under newspapers and tattered, worn coats; rats scurried over motionless bodies; the sound of sirens echoed in the distance, police sirens.

She shook her head, regaining some of the lost clarity, shaking away the shadows. Her vision sharpened.

A hand held hers; a rough, arthritic, dry, callused hand that reminded her of someone. Sadie?

Her last safe place, her last foster mother, the cook from the Home who took her away from that depressing, unforgiving place to give her a real home, the first she had known in some time.

Sadie? She dared hope in her semi-conscious state.

Even knowing the risks, knowing her life's story, Sadie had taken her in; in spite of the dangerous truths that came with the young girl's past, Sadie dared to love her.

A smile grew within the girl's heart; a buoyant bubble burst by a moment of memory.

This was not the hand of Sadie holding hers. It couldn't be Sadie's hand, because Sadie was dead.

Guilt flooded her, chasing out the smile of hope, spreading to every chilly limb—tiny bottle rockets exploding beneath her skin—returning the trembling to her body after the darkness had left it warm and forgotten.

Flashes of Sadie, the short time they spent together as a family, replayed in her mind in various minuscule moments.

Sirens in the background; the little apartment Sadie shared with her.

Six months of memories replayed like old movie scenes, short clips leading to the last time she saw Sadie, lying on the kitchen floor, coffee cup shattered, shards spread atop dark spots that speckled the linoleum, as if the older woman's own skin had been cast in various sized pieces among the kitchen. Sadie's death was her fault, just like all the others who had tried to love her.

The camera of her mind replayed the image of her own body running out the front door, away from the scene of death, death she caused, wearing only the pajamas in which she had awakened that morning, a budding actress fleeing the suspense thriller that was her life.

She shook the memories away; her burning eyes blinked to check the tears that always followed; her body racked with shivers.

Someone sitting before her repeated the same words over and over; a dry, croaking voice echoed into the depths of her inner ear; someone else unashamedly dripped his own hot tears on her big toe, its hiding place given away by a hole in a trashcan, cross trainer.

She let her eyes move up from the hands joined before her, over the arms, across the face of the old woman standing there, to rest upon the young, rough looking boy; a toboggan fitted over the crown of his head; greasy golden spikes poked out over his too large ears; baggy, ripped clothes hung on his body; dry, cracked lips moving; tiny streams followed two freckled white lines down a dirt-encrusted face, drip... drip... drip.

"Thank you!" His thin arms reached out to her; his dry hands, palms partially concealed by time worn gloves, rested on her boney shoulders, as if to pull her into a hug.

She tried to shrug away, but his hands gripped her shoulders firmly while tears continually splattered her toe. "Thank you for bringing him to me, my little brother..." His voice broke with emotion.

Cheater searched beyond the old woman, the boy, her eyes questioning. Him who? What brother? Without success, her eyes sought another boy, the one he mentioned.

Why this tobogganed boy was so grateful she didn't understand; she never understood.

She... or something... changed people this way every time the darkness came. No memories of heroic acts remained.

Although no visible reuniting of family members presented itself, each spoke of another family member, as if she had pulled them from the depths of Hell and returned each to their long lost brother, mother, sister, aunt, uncle, spouse, but all she knew, all she remembered, was the darkness; all she ever remembered was the darkness.

From a pool of Sunday school memories, she learned that Hell was a dark place, but it was also filled with flames, so Hell couldn't possibly compare to the total darkness she encountered, no matter how warm she felt when stashed away there; it was a different type of warmth, a safe warmth, an infant swaddled in blankets and loving arms warmth.

And the people, the admiration, the changes, the after effects of the darkness, she remembered those. Not knowing what happened or where she went during these mindless times scared her as much as the faceless man dream ever did.

Sirens ripped the morning air.

Closer!

Louder!

They shrieked through her thoughts. The dog yipped his warning. He understood.

She looked down at the homeless woman, gray hair sticking up about her drawn face, a bruise darkening her left cheek, one hand holding a dented, half full can of black label green beans.

Standing beside the old woman, the young man, his face frozen in that look of awe, still spoke, "Thank you."

Every blackout left her in the same scene, different people, and different places.

Every time she blacked out, the same ending, changes for the better.

"I'll make it up to you. I promise." She heard as she tore herself from them. "I'm going to get a job, somehow, somewhere, take care of both of us. I don't have anyone e..." Cheater fled; she couldn't listen; she had to run. The sirens were too close. She couldn't chance the police catching her; they continued to search for her, missing person posters up on every corner, on every wooden pole, some now only corners of paper stuck to staples, ones she had ripped from their perches.

They'd take her away if they caught her, take her back; she couldn't go back, because this time they would send her to a worse place.

She had a mission to accomplish first. She had to find him, the faceless man, and she couldn't do it locked up in a youth home or a correctional facility.

She ran, an out of place gazelle bounding down the dirty city sidewalk, wiry frame leaping tumbled trash cans, fire hydrants, small animals— the sirens closer, the little dog padding behind.

She breezed past a restaurant with the King's face in neon sticking out over the roof of the building, soles slapping the cracked concrete.

The King smiled down at her, mocking her from above the outdoor tables where half-eaten food littered two or three of the bolted down wrought iron surfaces, the aroma from within calling her stomach to breakfast.

Cheater grabbed hopefully at a slightly crumpled bag left behind, the newspaper stand worker just rising from the table and walking back to his job, his disgust for the cheap meal apparent.

As she ran by him, she prayed he would ignore her, that she wouldn't be caught, that she wouldn't trip over the soles of her old sneakers as they gaped with each slap against the concrete. The little dog ran at her heels, ears bouncing, curled tail stiff.

About the Author

Gean Penny (aka P.G. Shriver) lives on a small horse farm in Texas with her family. She has been writing since the age of seven and to date has eleven books published, nine under Gean Penny and two under P. G Shriver.

Following an eight-year career teaching middle school, Gean returned to teaching at the college level. Some of her hobbies are gardening, reading, sewing, horseback riding and traveling.

Gean is currently working on The Lost Prince, the third book in the trilogy *The Gifted Ones Trilogy*, written under the name P.G. Shriver. Visit her website to share your thoughts or questions on Moon Thief, or any of the other books she has written. She would love to hear your opinions or questions.

Watch for several more young reader's books from this author in the future.

Visit her webpage at www.pgshriver.com for more information about her and to see more of her books.

Remember, if you enjoyed Moon Thief, please post a review at the following links:

https://www.amazon.com/dp/1712581201/

r#customerReviews
https://www.facebook.com/AuthorPGShriver/
reviews
https://www.barnesandnoble.com
http://www.goodreads.com

Follow this author at

Https://www.patreon.com/pgshriver
https://www.amazon.com/-/e/B006UL4BJO
https://www.amazon.com/-/e/B007B2MAPS

CPSIA information can be obtained
at www.ICGtesting.com
Printed in the USA
BVHW041115100720
583432BV00010B/92